THE
GEOMANCER'S COMPASS

THE
GEOMANCER'S
COMPASS

Melissa Hardy

TUNDRA BOOKS

Published in Canada by Tundra Books,
a division of Random House of Canada Limited,
One Toronto Street, Suite 300, Toronto, Ontario M5C 2V6

Published in the United States by Tundra Books of Northern New York,
P.O. Box 1030, Plattsburgh, New York 12901

Library of Congress Control Number: 2011938775

LIBRARY AND ARCHIVES CANADA CATALOGUING IN PUBLICATION

Hardy, Melissa
The geomancer's compass / by Melissa Hardy.

ISBN 978-1-77049-292-9. – ISBN 978-1-77049-365-0 (EPUB)

I. Title.

PS8565.A63243G46 2012   jC813'.54   C2011-906507-X

We acknowledge the financial support of the Government of Canada
through the Canada Book Fund and that of the Government of Ontario
through the Ontario Media Development Corporation's Ontario Book
Initiative. We further acknowledge the support of the Canada Council for
the Arts and the Ontario Arts Council for our publishing program.

ONTARIO ARTS COUNCIL
CONSEIL DES ARTS DE L'ONTARIO

Design: Jennifer Lum

www.tundrabooks.com

Printed and bound in the United States of America

1 2 3 4 5 6   17 16 15 14 13 12

For my brother and
fellow voyageur in the realms of fantasy,
Peter Hardy

"Nothing is exactly as it seems.
Nor is it otherwise."

N<small>ANCY</small> B<small>ODWIN</small>, *Weeds*

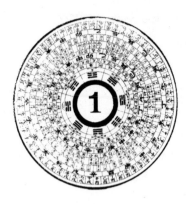

The first clue I got that there was something up with my family was just after I had been accepted at St. Izzy's in 2018. I had just turned thirteen, a dish served with all the trimmings – acne, braces, hair where before there had been none, and a big dollop of angst on the side. I remember it pretty clearly, despite the hormonal haze. There's my post-tweeny, pre-adolescent self, all five feet and one hundred pounds of it, supercharged on too much Guarana Fizz. I'm barreling down the big front hall in the house on Pender Street on track to scoring more to rocket boost me through some Extreme Calculus homework. That's when I overhear my A-Ma – that's Chinese for paternal grandmother – talking about my great-great-grandfather's funeral arrangements with my mother and aunt in the living room. He had choked to death on a moon cake two and a half weeks before. What she said was this: "You do know he was born in the back room of a hand laundry in Moose Jaw, don't you?" Which was a shock. I'd never paid much attention to old family stuff. Trust me, it was like peering into a swamp – stinky with lots of strange creatures that you could barely make out, just swimming around – but I'd always thought the old man had been born in Vancouver, like the rest of us, not in the boonies somewhere.

"What year was that?" This from my Auntie Ev.

"The Year of the Sheep," A-Ma replied.

Chinese people always talk about what year you were born in. It's like the zodiac, only with years instead of months. You don't say, "What's your sign?" You say, "What year are you?" For example, I was born in 2005, the Year of the Rooster, which is supposed to make me a workaholic who's not afraid to speak my mind, so there you go. Not that I believe that stuff.

"Wasn't that the same year the Canadian Pacific Railway was completed?" my mother asked.

A-Ma shook her head. "No, he was born the previous year."

I poked my head in the door. "Wrong! The last spike was driven in November 1885." Three heads swiveled in my direction.

"Miranda! I thought you had homework," my mother said.

"My life is homework," I told her. "That's how I know that the CPR was completed in 1885. We just finished our transportation module last week."

"And?"

"Do the math." I crossed over to a Ming-style armchair and plopped myself down. "It's 2018. If the railroad was completed in 1885 and The Grandfather was born a year earlier, he'd have been a hundred and thirty-four years old when he died."

We always referred to my great-great-grandfather, Liu Xiazong, a.k.a. Charlie Liu, as *The* Grandfather, with an emphasis on the "The." This had served originally to distinguish him from my grandfather, Ye-Ye, and my great-grandfather, Jeng-Ye, both of whom he had survived by many years. He had been the patriarch, after all, *The* Patriarch, and Chinese people are all about the patriarch – Chinese Canadians too, especially first- and second-generation ones. And you had to hand it to the old guy. The first of his family born on Canadian soil, he had pretty much single-handedly amassed the family fortune and founded the Liu dynasty, such as that was. The Grandfather was, in short, a big cheese. And not just as far as his family went. The whole Chinese-Canadian community in Vancouver looked up to him. He'd practically run the Chinese Benevolent Association for decades.

"A hundred and thirty-four years old," A-Ma repeated. She nodded. "That sounds right."

"But that's impossible," I said. "Nobody lives to be that old. Not with all the toxins and superbugs. Not with the ozone layer in shreds. Not with *germs*." (I have a tiny problem with germs; I don't trust them, and they are *everywhere*.)

"People in Georgia frequently live to be over one hundred," Auntie Ev piped up from her wheelchair. Before her illness, she played second viola with the Vancouver Symphony Orchestra; now her hands shook too much for her to hold a viola, much less play it. "The Republic of Georgia, that is, not the American state. It has to do with their diet. Apparently they eat a lot of yogurt."

"C'mon, Auntie Ev," I said. "Living to over a hundred and living to a hundred and thirty-four are very different – like unusual versus impossible."

She deflated into glumness, tucked away there in her dark corner of the living room. She had eaten yogurt until it came out her ears, had tried everything, but nothing the slew of doctors and specialists and naturopaths and traditional Chinese medicine practitioners recommended had restored her body to her, or even slowed her rapid slide into paralysis. It was beyond depressing.

"I know it's unusual to live as long as The Grandfather," A-Ma said, "but sometimes people whose life's work is incomplete find that they must live longer than others; that they need more time to . . . to wrap things up."

My A-Ma's name was Lin, which means "Beautiful Jade" in Chinese; it suited her, even though she was old. She was the most self-contained, most serene person I had ever known. Utterly Zen-like. She ran the household on Pender Street – and it was huge – like it was nothing at all and tended to our ramshackle and accident-prone family with an air of quiet competence. I'd seen A-Ma upset; I'd seen her sad; but I'd never seen her rattled. I had the feeling that if I ever did, if any of us ever did, we'd panic, come apart at the seams. She was that steady. At the time, of course, I thought she was being ridiculous and pigheaded.

"Oh, come on. What didn't he do? He did everything!"

Because Charlie Liu's achievements were the stuff of legend, at least in the Chinatown I grew up in. He had started out importing and canning Hong Kong opium; then, when trading in opium became illegal, he imported tea and silk and Chinese medicines instead, all the while investing in real estate, both in Chinatown and in the growing city of Xianshuibu, Brackish Water Port, the Chinese name for Vancouver. The company he founded, Azure Dragon Imports, takes up an entire corner of Chinatown and offers customers everything from calligraphy sets to paper lanterns, from *mah-jongg* tiles to silk *cheongsams*, from jade and coral jewelry to statues of the Buddha. And our house – twenty-two rooms built around three courtyards – is more like a small palace than a private home. I mean, you can get lost in there. Trust me.

"He was very successful," A-Ma agreed. "But even a successful man can have unfinished business."

"Mother Liu." Mom's tone was sharp, startlingly so. She usually deferred to A-Ma. Everybody did. But now she scowled at her, raised her eyebrows pointedly, and gave her head a little shake, like she was forbidding her to do something, warning her. She turned to me. "The Grandfather lived as long as he did because of his diet, Miranda. Period. End of story. Rice and a little fish."

"And moon cakes." Auntie Ev sounded rueful. "Let's not forget the moon cakes."

I wrinkled up my nose. Heavy and not very sweet, moon cakes are round pastries filled with lotus-seed paste and salted egg yolks. Not my idea of a yummy treat, but The Grandfather loved them; they were his absolute favorite thing, and he looked forward every year to the Mid-Autumn Moon Festival when he could eat his fill of the nasty things. Ever since he had lost his teeth back in the 1950s, the women of the family had been terrified that he would choke on a pastry, and with good reason. Then, this year, bingo. Dead at the alleged age of a hundred and thirty-four. Death by Cantonese delicacy.

And then this weird exchange took place between my grandmother and my mother, conducted in a kind of hiss, but still perfectly audible. I mean, I was sitting only a few feet away and, despite how loudly I played my tunes even then, I wasn't deaf.

"Daisy." A-Ma leaned over to tug at Mom's sleeve. "You know full well the child has to know sometime."

Mom shook her head. "Not now, Mother Liu."

"But we all agree that –"

"I said no. She is too young."

"But we don't know how much time –"

"*I said she is too young.*"

I leaned forward in my chair. "Hey. *Apollo* to Houston. I'm in the room, you know. What are you talking about? What is it that I have to know?"

A-Ma looked at Mom. Mom scowled, crossed her arms over her chest, and shook her head once again. A-Ma shrugged. "All right," she said, turning away. "As you wish."

"I am her mother."

"You are."

"And you don't know, Mother Liu. The situation might change. Right itself."

"That is unlikely, Daisy, and you know it."

"Nonetheless."

"What is going on? What are you talking about?" I demanded, but neither of them would say a word more on the subject. They just sat there with their zipped lips, so I eventually gave up and went back to my original plan to raid the fridge. Time passed and, in the commotion and chaos generated by The Grandfather's funeral, I would probably have forgotten all about this conversation, or non-conversation, if it hadn't been for what happened at the cemetery.

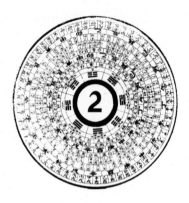

The Grandfather's funeral was five hours long, start to finish – in other words, interminable. A white hearse led the procession up the winding road along the waterfront to the cemetery where Vancouver's Chinese-Canadian community had buried their dead since the 1930s. Through its tinted windows, passersby could just make out the yellow-lacquered casket, nailed shut, in which The Grandfather's dry leaf of a body rested. I knew from A-Ma that he was wearing the burial garments he had chosen in 1949 on his sixty-fifth birthday. Since that time, these garments had lain, carefully wrapped in muslin, in the carved camphor trunk at the foot of the narrow, red-lacquered bed in which he had slept since the death of his wife six decades earlier.

It was a balmy autumn day, not raining for once, unusual for Vancouver. The air was soft and hazy, and a brisk wind bustled around like an old auntie telling everyone to hurry along, hurry along now. The two teenage sons of Donald Chen, the Chinese undertaker, walked behind the hearse, lackadaisically swirling paper streamers. They were older than me but, in spite of that, they still managed to be completely lame. Maybe all undertakers' children are lame; maybe it goes with the turf. In any case, every few minutes they would jump up and down on the streamers, whooping half-heartedly. Probably they would have preferred to be home playing Mass Driver or World of Starcraft (I know I would have), but I'll bet their dad insisted that they be there, doing their streamer gig. He knew his customers – knew that, for old-school Chinese, streamers were an essential element of any funeral. "How do you think I pay for your fancy video games?" he'd ask them. "Where do you think the money for those expensive cross-trainers comes from?" Chinese-Canadian parents are all alike. They want you to know how much things cost.

Behind the boys crept the white limousine in which A-Ma and I traveled. Of her six grandchildren, A-Ma had chosen me and only me to join her in the lead car (my mom and dad and two brothers followed in another, lesser car, farther back in the procession). I remember being puzzled by this, and a little weirded out. In Chinese-Canadian families, all hopes for the future are usually pinned on the male heir. This meant that, by rights, one of my brothers or male cousins should have been chosen to sit with A-Ma – probably my cousin Brian, who is a few months older than me. Any of the other kids might have felt proud at being singled out; I felt uneasy. The last thing in the world I wanted was to be The Heir, to have all those family and company responsibilities dumped into my lap. I had my future all mapped out and it was going to be great. St. Izzy's is this insanely difficult private academy with a mission to produce the next generation of computer geniuses. By getting accepted there, I had put myself on a super fast track to work in some of the new markup and metadata languages being developed for Web3D – high-tech, high-level stuff about which my family had no clue – and I didn't want anything to get in the way of my plans.

A-Ma pinched me on the arm – not hard. "You're fidgeting," she snapped. "Stop it." She looked very small and neat in her short-sleeved Chinese pantsuit with its mandarin collar and frog buttons. Both her suit and the *cheongsam* that Mom had insisted I wear were made of white silk brocade. For Chinese people, white is the color of mourning, not black like it is for most Canadians.

"It's this stupid dress," I complained. "It's itchy." I'd always been more of a jeans girl – a tomboy who, upon hitting puberty, quickly morphed into a nerd. I wasn't used to wearing a dress, especially one with such a narrow skirt. "How are you expected to walk in this thing?"

"Take little steps."

I squirmed, tugging at the tight mandarin collar, which was chafing me. "How do you run?"

She gave a little hoot. "You don't."

I scowled at the Chen brothers. I am, by nature, both prickly and finicky, and physical discomfort only makes that worse. "What do those two nimrods think they're doing? They look totally pathetic."

"Now, Miranda, they are doing an important job."

"Yeah? What?"

"They are entangling devils." She said this as calmly as she might have said, "They are eating freezer pops."

This flabbergasted me. "What did you say?"

"I said they are *entangling devils*."

I snorted. "Yeah, sure."

"They are."

"A-Ma. You've got to be kidding me."

My grandmother only shook her head. "I am being perfectly serious."

"Devils?"

"Devils."

"It's symbolic, right? Traditional?"

"Traditional," said A-Ma. "But not symbolic."

I sighed. Every year it seemed she became more traditional, more conservative, more *Chinese.* Even her speech had begun to sound slightly accented, as though English might have been her second language, even though she was second-generation

British Columbian. And she was educated. She had traveled. It wasn't as though she were some peasant from a small village in China. "There are no such things as devils, A-Ma. You know that."

"I do not," she said. "And if you saw what I have seen in my long life, you would think differently."

I believed in progress, in science and technology. I believed in germs. Want to believe in something scary that you can't see? Germs beat out devils every time. I didn't understand why my grandmother felt so compelled to preserve the old traditions, why she was so superstitious, especially when she knew, or *ought* to have known, better.

Take the past several weeks leading up to the funeral, while we waited (and waited) as old Dr. Yu, the geomancer, hemmed and hawed, trying to find a day that, astrologically speaking, was not fraught with danger for the family. How crazy was that?

And what about the household gods, all those garishly painted statues of deities and sitting Buddhas and Confucian figures that littered the house? A-Ma had insisted that they all be covered with red cloth, but that no one should wear red clothing. Red was a happy color, and funerals were sad.

She had also insisted that all the mirrors be removed from sight, and that a white cloth be hung in the front doorway. When I asked about the mirrors, she told me that if anyone saw The Grandfather's yellow-lacquered coffin in a mirror, there would surely be another death in the family right away. As for the white cloth hanging in the doorway, all I could get out of her was "That is how it must be done. Otherwise there will be ill fortune."

It would be one thing if it was just cultural, a case of going through the motions. That would have been quaint or charming or something. What bugged me was that she really seemed to believe she could stave off disaster only by observing these ancient rites. It was nuts. And I have to admit I have little tolerance for stupid people, not being one myself. That my beloved A-Ma (because I really did love her) should *act* like a stupid person, especially when I knew she was not one, was super-annoying.

"Anything you may think you've seen, A-Ma, there's a scientific explanation for," I told her. "Besides, even if there were devils, what would they be doing at an old man's funeral?"

Now, here comes the "oh snap" moment. Are you ready for it?

"They are here to attack The Grandfather," she said. "He was their enemy in life and now they want revenge. He made them wait a long time and they are very angry at him."

Now, The Grandfather had been around my whole life, but to tell you the absolute truth he hadn't seemed like a person so much as a family heirloom, something that was taken out and dusted off and prominently displayed at the head of a table or in the place of honor at some ceremony.

His English was heavily accented, despite his having been born in Canada, and in any case he rarely spoke, at least in my presence, and then in such a hoarse whisper that it was difficult to make out what he was saying. It was like his words were trying to escape through a tangle of barbed wire clogged with debris. I had always assumed he was senile. How could you be that old and *not* senile? But senile or not, he hadn't seemed like the sort of person anyone or any*thing* would target for attack. What would be the point?

"Oh, come on," I said. "I find that hard to believe."

"You knew him only as a very old man," said A-Ma. "Past his prime. Believe me when I tell you that in his day he was a fierce warrior, and devils are bound and determined to get him now, when he is most vulnerable."

"Vulnerable? He's dead. What does he have to lose?"

"His body may be dead, but his soul is not at rest," she said. "It is neither here nor there. It is confused. When it is in this state, it may become lost, perhaps forever."

"OK," I bargained. "Let's say that devils are gunning for The Grandfather's soul – I'm speaking hypothetically here – then why the streamers? Are devils scared of streamers?" An image of little red devils with horns and barbed tails and pitchforks, cowering before a paper streamer, popped into my mind. I laughed. "Because anything that's scared of a streamer . . . well, that's not something I'd lose a lot of sleep over."

"You see the holes in the streamers?"

I squinted. Sure enough, the streamers were pierced with many tiny holes. "Yeah? So?"

"The devils must pass through each one of those holes to get to The Grandfather. Like running a gauntlet. The Chen boys are keeping them busy, distracting them . . ."

One of the boys stomped. "Yow," he yodeled.

"See? He just crushed one."

Exasperated, I closed my eyes and fell back against the seat. "That's totally crazy."

"Crazy?"

"As in: can you show me where it is written down that a devil has to pass through holes in order to get to its victim?"

"Devils are just as bound by custom and tradition as we are."

"Not."

"They are."

"Oh, come on, A-Ma. Are you saying there's some sort of rule book governing how devils and human beings interact?"

"There is an understanding . . ."

"The representatives of mankind and the devils' union sat down and wrote up an agreement – devils could attack people, but only after they'd passed through x number of holes . . ."

"Miranda, don't be disrespectful. I said there is an understanding. A cosmic understanding."

"Oh, A-Ma, admit it. Even if there were devils, what could they do to hurt The Grandfather? He's dead. Surely he's beyond help or harm."

She shook her head. "That is not true, granddaughter. Remember that although the many worlds of incarnation make up the foreground of existence, in order to have a foreground you must also have a background – the space between worlds, the place we call the Bardo."

Whoa. The Bardo? What on earth was she talking about?

She tried a different tack. "Think of the night sky, Miranda. The stars are the many worlds and the Bardo is the night sky, in which the stars hang. The Grandfather's soul is now in the Bardo, the space between his death and his eventual rebirth into a different form. How a soul fares in the Bardo will greatly influence the form his rebirth takes. That's why we will hold a prayer ceremony for his soul every ten days – so that he will be reborn into this world and not one of the other worlds. If the devils turn him into an *iau-kuai*, however, all our efforts will be in vain."

"Into a what?"

"An *iau-kuai*. A powerful monster."

"Like they can do that."

"Well, they can. I know you think I'm a foolish old woman, but there are many things you don't yet understand."

"How you can believe in devils and monsters? This is the twenty-first century, not the Han dynasty." I paused. "So, what do these *iau-kuais* look like?"

"Like a seething whirlwind of teeth, claws, dust, and rags," she replied. "They have fierce orange eyes that glow like embers. Sometimes they make terrible booming noises like something you'd hear in space; other times they squeak like bats. They blow about the earth, gobbling up their victims."

"And how do they kill these victims?"

"Why, they frighten them to death," A-Ma exclaimed. "Wouldn't you be frightened if you saw such a dreadful creature?"

"Yeah," I said. "If such a creature existed. WHICH IT DOESN'T."

Later, at the grave site, a pair of The Grandfather's red silk embroidered shoes, his glossy black skullcap, and a pair of hand-carved wooden chopsticks were burned in the brick funeral burner, along with a big basket of yellow and white holy paper.

"Why are they doing that?" I asked.

"He will need a few things in his new life," A-Ma said. With a straight face.

The air grew thick with the odor of incense and the smell of burning Chinese herbs and roasted meat – a white Cadillac heaped high with roast chickens and a whole roasted pig and wooden baskets of oranges and apples had followed the funeral procession to the cemetery. Women went through the motions of wailing and shrieking (it was expected that they do this, especially given The Grandfather's great wealth – the richer the deceased, the louder and longer the wailing); boys set off firecrackers and men banged on gongs and drums – to scare off demons, of course. All that shrieking and carrying on was giving me a massive headache, that and the fact that my mom had braided my hair way too tight.

A-Ma tugged at my elbow. "See that little Guan boy?" She glanced pointedly beyond the holy burner to a cluster of bushes in which six-year-old Nigel Guan stood, trying to look non-chalant, as though he were not, in fact, peeing. "A ghost will follow him home and torture him with illness. Mark my words."

"Demons. Ghosts. I thought this was supposed to be an auspicious day," I grumbled.

"That only means that there are no monsters about. As for evil spirits and ghosts, they are always with us."

I snorted.

A-Ma frowned. "I can see them," she said. "One day you will see them too. They are all around us. They are everywhere."

I didn't believe her, of course, but it still creeped me out.

What was with her? I wondered. For some reason she was pulling out all the crazy old-school Chinese stops today – all directed toward me. And so intense. Why did I have to accompany her? I wasn't the boy. I wasn't the Chosen One.

The Taoist priest circulated among the mourners, passing out *poot jai gou*, steamed cakes made of red dates and glutinous rice flour. *Poot jai gou* falls into the same food group as moon cakes – the dense, sticky, sketchy tasting food group. When the priest got around to me, I tried to say no, but A-Ma insisted I take one. She watched me like a hawk while I ate it, and afterward made me stick out my tongue to prove I had swallowed the nasty mess. "Red wards off evil spirits," she lectured me, waggling her finger. "Always remember that."

"I thought red was a happy color," I grumbled. Under my breath I said, "Make up your mind!"

Later, when the wailing had stopped and everyone was packing up to go home, A-Ma and I were standing at the head of the grave, looking out at the Pacific. Mom was with the rest of the family, some distance away, out of earshot. That's when it happened, when A-Ma told me what she had started to tell me that day in the living room, what Mom didn't want me to know because she thought I was too young. Taking me by the arm, she drew me near. "You don't think there are evil spirits?" she whispered. "Look at our family if you want proof of their power and their hatred toward us."

"What are you talking about?"

"I mean it," she warned. "Look. Look at them, Miranda."

I glanced around the funeral party.

There was Dad. Five years ago he had been struck by lightning on a golf course. As a result of this, he was, as Mom put it, "a shattered man." He sat at the side of the grave, twitching occasionally and mumbling, in a lawn chair brought for the purpose. It was lucky that we were rich because the doctors couldn't tell us whether Dad would ever work again or be the way he was before the accident – strict but kind of goofy too, always telling what he called Dumb Dad Jokes and tickling you.

My five-year-old brother, Liam, was nestled on his lap. Liam was . . . well, Liam was pitiful. I don't know how else to say it. Limp and small for his age, he had trouble catching his breath, which meant he couldn't play or go to a normal school or anything. He always looked kind of blue, and his life was a round robin of respiratory therapy and oxygen treatments and visits to doctors who couldn't figure out what the problem was.

Beside Dad stood Sebastian, my ten-year-old brother, who for some reason nobody could explain was losing his eyesight and, beside him, looking drawn and exhausted, Mom. She had felt mysteriously tired for the last couple of years and lately had begun to experience muscle pain in many parts of her body – neck, spine, shoulder, hips, and ankles.

And of course there was Auntie Ev, my father's sister, wheelchair-bound, and her son Brian – the one who should have accompanied A-Ma in the lead car. Powerfully built and with extreme hair, Brian had severe dyslexia – try as he might, he just couldn't learn to read. He also had ADHD – Attention Deficit Hyperactivity Disorder – which meant that he couldn't sit still and had the attention span of a Mexican jumping bean. He was four months my senior. At that moment he was darting around the cemetery, staring uncomprehendingly at the writing on the headstones. He was probably trying to find his father's grave. Auntie Ev's husband, Phil, had been killed in a freak accident two years earlier. A falling icicle had pierced his jugular vein when he was walking home from the hospital where he was a surgeon. As for Auntie Ev's other children, Oliver and Aubrey, they were not at the funeral. Eighteen-year-old Oliver was being treated for agoraphobia – a fear of going out in public – at a private clinic on the Sunshine Coast, while sixteen-year-old Aubrey was being intravenously fed at an exclusive eating disorders clinic in Victoria. When she had entered the clinic two months earlier, she had stood five foot eight and weighed eighty-four pounds.

"A lot of bad things seem to have happened to us lately," I admitted. "But things are going to get better. I know they are. They just have to."

The old woman rolled her eyes heavenward and shook her head. "Miranda, you surprise me. As bright as you are. So it's really never occurred to you that the Lius might be cursed?"

Talk about coming from left field. "Cursed?"

"Cursed."

"As in *The Curse of the Mummy's Tomb* cursed?"

She nodded.

"Wow."

I noticed that Mom was watching us. She did not look happy. Frowning, she bent down and said something to Dad, who blinked up at her, his face slack. Then she walked over to where we stood. "What are you two talking about?" she asked suspiciously. "Mother Liu?"

"Such a good concentration of cosmic breaths here," replied A-Ma, a little too quickly. "The excellent *yang* of that hill behind us, the way the *chi* flows . . . naturally, Miranda thinks it's all bunk. Don't you?" She looked pointedly at me and I understood that I was being invited to conspire with her against my mother.

"Honestly, A-Ma," I managed. "Cosmic breaths?"

"Well, I for one know that The Grandfather's spirit will be happy in this place," A-Ma concluded, giving me the tiniest little smile by way of condoning my treachery. "He should give us no trouble. *Not like the other one.*"

"Mother Liu." The warning in Mom's tone was unmistakable.

"Other one?" I asked. "What other one?"

Mom went into hyper-bustle mode. "Come, Mother Liu. Come, Miranda. I don't know about you, but I'm exhausted.

And it's time for Liam's physio. Chop-chop." Taking A-Ma by one arm and me by the other, she marched us toward the white cavalcade of cars with a look on her face as grim as the Reaper's.

And that was that.

Only it wasn't.

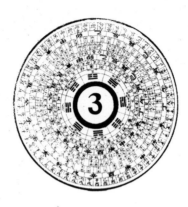

Three years later, Mom called me in Calgary and told me that A-Ma was dying and I'd better get myself home fast, because she didn't have long and she'd asked for me. "There's something important she wants to tell you."

"What? What could she want to tell me?" I begged.

The news that A-Ma was sick, never mind *dying*, had sent my brain into complete free-fall. How could my grandmother die? She had always been the strong one, the rock, our island of calm, the fixed star by which we navigated our various leaky boats. I couldn't conceive of a world without her in it. I didn't want to even try.

"How should I know?" Mom said shortly. I could tell from her tone that she did know, that she was lying. She always sounds angry when she's lying, like she's mad that she has to and it's somehow your fault. "I've booked you out of Calgary on Air

Canada flight 225, leaving at 6:20 tonight. Can you make that?"

I glanced at my watch. I could barely make out the time through the tears welling up in my eyes. It was 4:50 in the afternoon – cutting it close. "Yeah. I guess. Sure."

The reason I was in Calgary was that I'd scored this wicked internship at CanBoard for the summer. CanBoard was the Canadian division of WorldBoard International, a consortium that had set out at the end of the 1900s to build a planetary infrastructure for associating digital information, tools, and services with a location, a person, or thing. In other words, Augmented Reality, or AR, where 3-D virtual objects are integrated into a real environment in real time. Totally, and I mean totally, cutting edge.

So I'd been living on my own out in Alberta for the past couple of months – well, on my own in a dorm, which is a little scary and lonely when you're sixteen and come from a big, tight-knit family, but also deeply cool, although it would have been cooler if I'd actually had any friends.

I realized Mom was still talking. I heard the words but I wasn't processing their meaning. My head was a jumble of thoughts about A-Ma, about my little, beautiful grandmother. I refocused with difficulty. "Don't go back to your dorm," Mom was saying. "Go straight to the airport and you'll make it in time. Are you listening? *Take a cab.*"

Later, just as the sun was beginning to set over the jagged, snowcapped peaks on three sides of the city of my birth, my cab pulled up in front of the house on Pender Street. No sooner had it stopped than the big front door opened a crack and Mom waved me in. She must have been watching from the window.

I paid the cab driver, then bounded up the front steps and into the house. "Mom!" I hadn't seen her since I had left for Calgary. Before the internship, the longest I'd ever been away from home on my own was a two-week computer camp. Seeing her, being home, I realized how much I had missed her. Seizing her hand, I squeezed it hard.

She gasped and pulled her hand quickly away.

"Oh." I said, remembering and wincing. "Sorry."

"No, honey, that's OK. Really."

What I'd forgotten was how hypersensitive she had become over the last few years. Practically any physical contact hurt her; we hadn't hugged for a long time. I could remember a time when she played tennis and was a champion swimmer. I could remember lots of hugs. But her sickness had eroded her the same way wind and water carve out shores and canyons – slowly, steadily, but most of all relentlessly. If you could hate a disease, I hated this one, whatever it was. It had taken the body of the mother I remembered, of the mother who could have been, and left in its wake one that was little more than the sum total of a thousand tiny points of agony. It was like she was its prisoner and it was never, ever going to let her go.

"Where's Daddy?" I asked, although I knew the answer already. He was doing what he always did: sitting in what used to be his home office, staring at the Window Wall – this huge TV taking up an entire wall that he had installed just before his accident. Not watching it. Staring at it. With empty eyes.

"In his office. Why? Do you want to see him?"

I shook my head quickly. What was there to see? "Maybe later."

No need to ask where the rest of them were. Sebastian was at some camp for blind kids up in the Interior and, by this time of day, Mom would have already strapped on Liam's mask nebulizer and helped him put on his chest wall oscillation vest for a long night of assisted breathing. As for the others, Auntie Ev had been dead for going on two years now. She had spent the last year of her life in bed, unable to lift her head off her pillow, begging for someone to kill her. It was pretty awful. My cousin Aubrey was in rehab for her eating disorder again – the last time I saw her, you could have threaded a needle with her – and Oliver was still at the clinic on the Sunshine Coast, which was sort of ironic since he never went outside. Only my cousin Brian was still a going concern. His combo of dyslexia and ADHD had made school difficult for him, but he had discovered a talent for torturing trees and had found a summer job he liked working for a commercial *bonsai* grower.

"A-Ma's in the little garden," Mom told me. "She's expecting you."

"Why don't you go and rest?" I said. She looked exhausted;
the bags under her eyes reminded me of a really sad basset
hound. "I know the way," I added.

She didn't argue. "OK," she said. "It's good that you're
home." She smiled wanly, then turned and dragged herself
up the stairs. I know it sounds weird to say that, but that's
what it looked like – like it was some super-steep hill and she
might not make it to the top.

I dropped my laptop and my knapsack by the door and
walked down the long, wide hall toward A-Ma's bedroom.
The garden was in a small, enclosed courtyard connected
to her room. I knocked tentatively, heard a faint "Come in,"
and pushed open the door. The room was only dimly lit.
I could just make out the brooding hulk of her big bed, built
out of cypress and covered with decorative carvings, and the
red and gold armoire in the corner, with its black frame and
butterfly decor handles. The lattice door to the courtyard
was open. I steeled myself, then crossed the bedroom and
walked out into the garden.

A winter-flowering plum stood at its center, its gnarled
branches reflected in the clear water of the little carp pool
beneath it. The flower beds that flanked the walls were planted
sparingly with wispy bamboo and miniature rhododendron.
Beside the pool were a pair of chairs, separated by a

glass-topped side table on which was placed a small cherrywood box. A-Ma reclined in one of these chairs, covered with an elaborately embroidered peacock-blue satin quilt, despite the warmth of the early August evening. Carp, fat and golden, slipped through the water like big drops of yellow oil, and the air was tangy with salt, the way it is in cities by the sea.

"A-Ma." I squatted down beside her chair and took her icy hand in mine. I squeezed it carefully – bird bones, skin as thin and brittle as a dried leaf. I was shocked at how fragile she had grown since I'd been in Calgary. It was like she was turning into a husk or something.

Her eyes creaked open a slit. "You came. I was hoping you would." Her voice was weak; she spoke in a faint whisper.

"Mom told me you weren't feeling well."

"She told you I was dying. . . . No, now shush." She lifted a trembling hand to silence my protests. "I told her to. Besides, it's true. You mustn't feel bad. I'm ready. I've lived eighty-four long years and now I'm tired. I want to be reborn into something young and sprightly. Something with a little sparkle."

"You look pretty sparkly to me." I smiled, but my eyes filled up with tears. "Besides, eighty-four is young. Look how old The Grandfather was when he died. And then only because he choked on a moon cake."

"Well, The Grandfather was a different case altogether," said A-Ma. "Help me to sit up a bit, will you?"

I cranked the chair to a more upright position.

"There now," she said, seeming to rally a little. "That's better. I've something for you." She pointed to the wooden box on the table.

I stood, reaching over her, and picked it up. It was maybe eight inches square, with intricately worked brass hinges and a symbol inlaid on its lid – mother-of-pearl and ebony. The symbol consisted of a circle equally divided into black and white sections by a reverse S-like shape. Within the black section was a small circle of white, and within the white section was a small circle of black. I recognized the symbol – it was the *yin-yang* symbol and you saw it all over Chinatown – but I couldn't remember what it meant, or maybe I'd never known. "Wow," I said. "This looks old."

"Go ahead," she said. "Open it."

Gingerly I opened the box and peered inside. I don't know what I expected – a jack-in-the-box? an explosive device? – but there, nestled in a lining of faded gold satin, was some sort of round instrument, about six inches in diameter, made of ivory. A smaller version of the *yin-yang* symbol on the lid appeared in the center of the instrument, surrounded by concentric rings densely inscribed with Chinese characters. "Cool," I breathed. "What is it?"

"A *lo p'an*," she replied. "*Lo* in Chinese means 'everything' and *p'an* means 'bowl.' The *lo p'an* is a circular bowl that holds all the mysteries of the earth. At least that's what The

Grandfather used to say. It's what they call a geomancer's compass."

I remembered Dr. Yu, the fumbling, fusty old geomancer with hair growing out of his ears, who had selected the date of The Grandfather's funeral based on the year, month, day, and hour of the old man's birth, using a Chinese almanac and something called a Heavenly Sixty-Four Hexagrams Chart. Ridiculous, of course, but according to A-Ma it had been totally important that the date be auspicious, which is to say lucky. If it wasn't auspicious, well, terrible things would supposedly happen. I remembered her description of monsters at The Grandfather's funeral, *iau-kuais*, seething whirlwinds of teeth, claws, dust, and rags with fierce orange eyes. "Was this Dr. Yu's?" I asked.

A-Ma smiled faintly and shook her head. "Dr. Yu? That old fool? No, this was The Grandfather's compass, Miranda . . . and his father's before him, and his grandfather's . . . and so forth and so on. This compass dates from the seventeenth century and was made, if memory serves me, in Quangdong Province, our ancestral home. The tradition, however . . . that goes back much further."

I have to admit that this took me by surprise. Given all his wheelings and dealings, The Grandfather must have been a pretty busy man in his day; not the kind of guy who had time for a lot of hobbies. "The Grandfather was a geomancer?"

A-Ma nodded. "He was. And his father and his grandfather. Of great renown. You come from a long line of geomancers." I think this was supposed to impress me.

"Really?" I said. "Well, what do you know? To tell you the truth, though, I haven't a clue what a geomancer does. I mean, other than event scheduling."

"Geomancy is an ancient and revered science," she replied. "It involves the identification and balancing of those subtle energies, or earth radiations, that disrupt our lives." She seemed more with it now than when I had first arrived. Her voice was stronger and the shaking had subsided. Maybe she had been asleep before and I had woken her up. "Which brings me to my point," she continued. "Why I asked for you. The Grandfather placed this compass in my safekeeping until such time as I could pass it on to you. That time has come."

This was a surprise. If I hadn't once thrown up on The Grandfather's birthday cake, I would have sworn that he didn't even know who I was. (He was jiggling me on his knee at the time, so really it was partially his fault; who does that to a kid who has already eaten her body weight in candy?) I mean, you'd think that two generations of grandchildren and great-grandchildren would all start to blur together after a while. But now he had left me this . . . I don't know what you'd call it . . . this precious family heirloom. He'd left it to me, specifically. "Wow," I began. "I'm *so* honored . . ."

A-Ma shook her head. "It is not a question of honor so much as obligation, Miranda. The Grandfather wanted you to safeguard the compass because of the mission you must undertake."

Suddenly I was beginning to get this bad feeling. And I mean *very* bad. "What mission?" I asked.

"The salvation of our family," she replied.

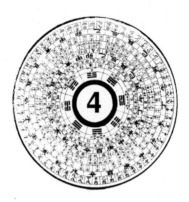

A flash of memory briefly lit up some distant corner of my brain as my mind jogged violently back in time – something locked away in RAM having to do with The Grandfather's funeral. "Is this about . . . the curse?" I asked.

She nodded.

"You think our family's cursed?"

"I know it is."

I sat back on my heels. "Well, in the first place, it isn't. That's just crazy. And, even if it was true, what would you expect me to do about it?"

"You must lift the curse," she replied. "That's your mission."

"Lift it? How?" I was beginning to feel kind of panicky. I didn't have time for some bogus mission. I had places to go, people to see. Well, not people to see, but metalanguages to write. "I'm a minor. Surely you've got to be a grown-up before you're allowed to go around lifting curses."

"This is serious, Miranda."

"No it's not. Not really. We may be a little dysfunctional –"

"Miranda!" she snapped. "Don't patronize me. And we are *not* dysfunctional. Families on sitcoms are dysfunctional. We are *doomed*." It was the first time she had ever raised her voice to me. I was so shocked I couldn't say a word. I just sat there, my bum on my heels, staring at her with my mouth hanging open. "Look," she continued, "I'm not the only one dying here. Our entire *family* is dying. All this illness . . . these accidents . . . you have to listen to me and do what I say. I haven't much time and, frankly, neither have you."

This took me aback. "What?"

"How long do you think it will be before something happens to you as well?" she demanded. "Some sort of cancer, or you just accidentally *happen* to fall down an elevator shaft?"

"*Excuse me?*"

She leaned forward in her chair and, reaching out, took my chin in her hand and stared deeply into my eyes. "I'm saying that you're the only Liu who has yet to be struck down. Do you think that's not going to happen? Why should you be spared?" She squeezed my chin, released it, and settled back in her chair, closing her eyes. This burst of activity, brief as it was, had clearly worn her out.

"I don't think about it, OK?" I stood. "It doesn't occur to me to worry about random things I can't control. That's being obsessive. That's being *crazy*."

She sighed and shook her head without opening her eyes. "I agree, Miranda. It is crazy. It's also true." She waved her hand in the air. "Oh, for heaven's sake, Miranda, will you just sit down and stop trying to talk me out of what I know, and let me explain?"

I shuffled over to the other chair and sat. I replaced the box containing the compass on the side table. "OK," I said. "Shoot."

A-Ma cleared her throat. "The reason why The Grandfather lived as long as he did was that he was waiting for you to grow up."

I shifted uncomfortably in the chair. "Me? Why me?"

"So that you could help him find a body."

"A body?"

"Well, more like bones."

"Bones?"

She nodded.

"What?" I asked. "Were they lost?"

"Terribly, tragically lost," she replied. "Unfortunately, The Grandfather choked on that moon cake before you were ready."

"Ready for what?"

"To help him," she said. "He knew that he would need

your technical skills if he was ever to find the body of Qianfu and lift the curse."

I held up my hand. "Hold on a minute. Who's Qianfu?"

"Qianfu was The Grandfather's twin brother," she replied. "He was beaten to death in the CPR rail yard in Moose Jaw in 1908."

Why had I never heard about this? "Wow. That's rough. Why?"

"It was passed off as a hate crime – there was a great deal of prejudice against the Chinese at that time, fear on the part of white men that the Chinese were taking their jobs. But that wasn't the real reason Qianfu was killed. It was because of Violet McNabb, a young woman who worked as a waitress in Wong's Chinese Restaurant. A *white* woman."

"And?"

"They fell in love."

"And that was such a crime?"

A-Ma smiled wearily. "At that time and in that place such a liaison was more than a crime, Miranda. It was . . . unspeakable, even unthinkable. It could be neither countenanced, nor forgiven. And he paid for it with his life."

"What happened to Violet?"

A-Ma dismissed my question with another wave of her hand. "Violet is beside the point. I think she married some pig farmer."

I whistled. "That's cruel and unusual punishment. Have you ever smelled a pig farm?"

"There's more to this than just a story of star-crossed lovers," A-Ma warned me. "Our family buried Qianfu, and after seven years his body was dug up and taken to the local Death House . . ."

I blinked. "The *what*?"

"The Death House," she replied matter-of-factly. "Where the bones of the deceased were scraped and whatever flesh remained on them was burned so that they could be returned to China and buried in our family graveyard in Zhongshan."

I shivered. "That's seriously creepy."

She shrugged. "It was the usual practice back then. Nobody wanted to be buried in a barbaric outback like Canada." I must have looked sort of green because she added, "What? Pumping corpses full of formaldehyde so they'll be preserved for perpetuity isn't creepy?"

"It's the creepy we know," I pointed out. "Go on."

"One cold winter night, the Death House caught on fire. When the firemen finally succeeded in putting out the flames, they discovered Qianfu's body. What was left of it, at any rate."

"And . . ."

"Moose Jaw went berserk," said A-Ma. "It hadn't been widely known that we twice-buried our dead. When white people found out, they exploded in outrage and horror. The local newspapers were full of it, riling up people, fanning the flames of hatred, of racism. Do you know how the editor of one of the local newspapers described the Chinese community?

As 'half-human, half-devil, rat-eating, rag-wearing, law-ignoring, Christian-civilization-hating, opium-smoking, labor-degrading, entrails-sucking celestials.' That's how."

I reflected on this for a moment. "'Entrails-sucking'? Really?"

She smiled faintly. "You can't make this stuff up. That was a bad time to be Chinese in Canada, Miranda. A very bad time. In any case, Alfred Humes, the town's chief of police, insisted on holding Qianfu's body, but refused to tell The Grandfather why. By the time a district court judge finally agreed to release the bones to The Grandfather, they had disappeared off the face of the earth. Clearly someone had gone ahead and disposed of them, but who and where? No one seemed to know . . . or, at any rate, no one was talking. Over the years, The Grandfather hired private investigator after private investigator. To no avail. To this day, we don't know where Qianfu's bones are."

I took a deep breath. "That sucks, A-Ma, but we're talking about bones here, not an actual person and, besides, the whole thing happened over a hundred years ago. It's over and done with. Why not let sleeping dogs lie?"

She shook her head. "If we only could. The cosmos doesn't work that way, Miranda. Sleeping dogs may lie, but not disgruntled ancestors. They roam. They cause trouble. And as our family has learned to its great sorrow, they can cover vast distances in pursuit of those they seek. The Grandfather moved his family here to Vancouver shortly after the terrible ordeal, but not even an entire mountain range has kept us safe from Qianfu's ghost."

I was beginning to put two and two together – curse, disgruntled ancestor, missing bones. "Let me get this straight: your theory is that Qianfu's ghost is hounding us from an unmarked grave somewhere on the Prairies? That he's the one responsible for all our problems?"

"It isn't a theory," she replied. "It's a fact."

"But why?" I asked. "Even if there are such things as ghosts, why would one go around attacking his own descendants for no good reason?"

"Clearly he is buried in a place with very bad *feng shui*," A-Ma replied. "And he doesn't like it one bit."

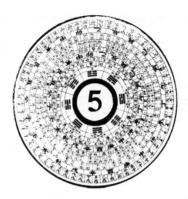

Feng shui?" I repeated. It was a Chinese term that had floated around my house attaching itself to this or that for as long as I could remember. What it actually meant I had no idea.

"*Feng shui* is the ancient Chinese practice of using the laws of heaven and earth to draw down positive *chi*," explained A-Ma. I must have looked blank because she continued, "*Chi* is essence – it's life force – oh, there's no word for it in English. Anyway, it's very important that a grave site have good *feng shui*. Like The Grandfather's. Its *feng shui* is excellent."

From my perspective, the best thing about The Grandfather's grave site had been its view of the ocean; maybe *feng shui* was just a fancy way of saying that. "But Qianfu's dead," I protested. "Why should he care about the view from his grave site? Why can't he just . . . I don't know . . . move on over or truck on down the road or go toward the light or something?"

"*Feng shui* is more than a view," she corrected me. (Well, scratch that theory.) "Don't you understand, Miranda? Souls are connected; families share karma. If a body is incorrectly laid to rest, it can't tap into beneficial *chi*, and that leads to great unhappiness for both the ancestor and his descendants. In Qianfu's case, this has resulted in his rebirth as an *e gui*."

"As a *what*?"

A-Ma looked sharply at me. "Geomancy, *feng shui*, *e guis* . . . That Chinese school we sent you to – did you learn anything there?"

A gut twist of guilt. "Not really," I confessed sheepishly. All us kids had been made to attend a Saturday-morning Chinese school when we were younger, so that we would know about Taoist beliefs and practices and Chinese culture in general. All of us but Oliver, that is; he wouldn't leave the house. I never understood how intelligent people living in the twenty-first century could believe in stuff like the Six Realms and the Wheel of Life, not to mention this whole wack of really lame gods like the Celestial Worthy of Numinous Treasure. (No, I'm not kidding; he was one of them.) Plus, doddering old Mr. Huang, who taught the class, was a one-man cure for insomnia, that singsong voice droning on and on. I could barely keep my eyes open. Besides, what's the use of learning something if it isn't true?

"I didn't think so." A-Ma sounded exasperated. Which

was unnerving, since she was, like, the soul of patience. "This is why we sent you to that school. So that I wouldn't have to explain these things to you now."

"Sorry," I apologized. "It was unbelievably boring."

"Nevertheless." She frowned. Her face was pinched; she looked like she was in pain. "All right, then. An *e gui* is a hungry ghost. If a spirit is unhappy, because it died badly or wasn't buried properly or has no descendants to perform the proper rituals, it is reborn as a hungry ghost. It has no recourse but to attack human beings if it wants its needs met. In the meantime it must feed, and that is what the ghost that was Qianfu has been doing for the past century – feeding on us, on our energy and our life force."

"Well, if his nose is so out of joint, why doesn't he show us where he's buried so we can dig him up and put him in some cooler place?"

"A hungry ghost is not a rational being, Miranda. It is nothing but a whirlwind of pain and desperate craving. You can't talk to one. You can't reason with one."

"Great. So how am I supposed to deal with this ecto-plasmic bummer?"

"You're not. Not alone, at any rate. Your mission is threefold – to safeguard the compass, to assist in finding Qianfu's body, and to provide technical support."

"Assist *whom*? Provide technical support *to whom*? And what do you mean by 'technical support'?"

She reached over and patted my hand. "All that will be revealed in due time."

"What do you mean?"

"Exactly what I said."

I played the age card. "I'm sixteen, A-Ma. How can I find a bag of bones buried in an unmarked grave a hundred years ago on the Prairies? I can't even drive."

"Well, that's where Brian comes in."

"Brian?"

"Yes, Brian. You remember Brian? Your cousin?" Now she was the one being sarcastic. "He's had his license for months now. You would have one too, if you had stopped studying long enough to take Drivers' Ed."

I was completely flummoxed. You have no idea how annoying Brian can be. "But he's . . . I mean, I love him and all, but he's a total goof."

"Oh, I understand that he's gotten quite good at digging up things," she said, almost blithely. "Trees and such. After all, somebody's got to dig up Qianfu and I somehow can't see you doing that. Oh, and before I forget . . ." She rummaged in a pocket of her housecoat and unearthed an old-fashioned key, intricately worked, black, and about two inches long. She handed it to me.

"And this is for . . . ?"

"The first locked door you encounter," she told me, closing her eyes. I noticed for the first time how transparent her eyelids were, like the thinnest of trembling membranes. Guilt washed over me. Here she was, dying maybe, and instead of humoring her so that she could go to her grave at peace, I was being my usual bullheaded self, refusing to give so much as an inch. Suddenly I felt like a toad, totally crappy.

She must have sensed my mood, because she patted my hand and, without opening her eyes, murmured, "Don't worry, granddaughter. I never expected you to accept what I had to tell you at face value. I know you, you see. I've known you all your life and it's simply not in your nature. Ever since you could speak, it's been one question after another – why, why, why? – and you're not satisfied until you get an answer. That's why we chose you – The Grandfather and I. Because you are curious and because you are relentless. Also, you are the only one capable of doing what is needed. I wish we could have waited until you were older, but there's no helping that." She squeezed my hand before releasing it. "Now, call my nurse and tell her to put me to bed. I'm tired." Mom had finally agreed to hire a live-in nurse to take care of A-Ma; it really upset Mom to have to do that, but it had become too much for her to manage, what with Dad and my brothers.

I slipped the key into my jeans pocket and stood. "I'll see you tomorrow."

She murmured something noncommittal in response. Bending down, I kissed her forehead lightly before sounding the brass gong for the nurse and stealing quietly from the darkening courtyard.

A-Ma died in her sleep that night and was buried a few days later on the left side of The Grandfather.

As the funeral was wrapping up and people were making their way to their cars through a light drizzle, I turned to Mom. "That plot to the right of The Grandfather . . . should we be thinking about buying it, maybe?" I was trying to sound mature and offhand, but it didn't come off that way – more like awkward and dorky.

She gave me a searching look, then swallowed and looked away, off toward the ocean, steel gray under a gray sky. "No need," she said. "It was bought and paid for a long time ago." She paused. "So . . . you know, then? She told you?"

"About the curse and the ghost?" I shrugged. "Yeah. She told me. Do I believe in that stuff? That's the real question."

"Do you?" She returned her gaze to me. The dark circles under her eyes looked like stains; they were the color of a ripening bruise. I would have assumed she knew the answer to that without having to think twice, but I was wrong. I read uncertainty in her look, and this was a woman who had graduated from university with an honors degree in Art History.

"Mom. Of course I don't believe in curses and ghosts. Do you?"

She shrugged. "Who knows? Maybe. There has to be some reason things have gone so badly for us, some explanation –"

"I agree," I interrupted her. "And it's a rational, scientific one." She looked so defeated and downhearted that my first impulse was to give her a big hug, but that would have made her feel like every bone in her body was broken and someone had poured gasoline over her and set her on fire. Instead I assured her, "I'll do my best to find Qianfu's bones. If that's even possible after so long. That much I promise. I'm not sure how much good it will do in the big scheme of things, but I'll do it."

"It's a lot to take on," Mom said. "Especially for someone so young. It's not what I wanted for you."

It's not what I wanted for myself, I thought grimly, but hey.

"When will you start?" she asked.

My jaw dropped. A-Ma hadn't said anything about a start-up time, not to my recollection. "What?"

"When will you be going to Moose Jaw?"

"Moose Jaw?"

"You'll have to go to Moose Jaw," she said. "I can book plane tickets for you and Brian."

Brian. Shit.

"Does he even know?" I asked. "Did A-Ma tell him?"

She shook her head. "Not yet. You know how he is, Miranda. We thought it best to wait until the time was right. So he wouldn't get into too much trouble in the meantime."

Great, I thought. Just what I need. A keg of dynamite with a short fuse.

"I don't know when I'll go," I said. "I haven't thought that far ahead." The truth was that I hadn't thought ahead at all. After all, when you're foggy about the *what* of something, it's pointless to decide on the *when*. "I've got to finish up my internship at CanBoard first . . . and then there's school starting up . . ."

"Miranda. You have to go sometime."

See, that was the operative idea: I had to go *sometime*. Not now. Not soon. But not never, either. Qianfu had been dead for over a century. Call me crazy, but I figured his ghost could probably wait until I graduated from high school before I went poking around Saskatchewan for his lousy grave. "Please, Mom. All this . . . it's a lot to take in all at once, and I can't just blow the CanBoard internship off. I can't. If I just up and leave, it would *so* not look good. This internship is really prestigious. People *kill* for this internship. You know that."

"All right," she said. "But after that."

"After that is school . . ."

"After that is a two-week break *before* school," she countered.

"A two-week break that is my only summer vacation . . ."

"Miranda." Her voice was shrill with anguish, her expression stricken. "You're not taking this seriously. You've got to understand. The rest of us . . . we're going downhill fast. It's getting worse and worse. With A-Ma gone, it's my job to hold this family together, and I don't know if I can, not when it's all I can do to get out of bed in the morning. You must do this and you must do it soon."

"All right, all right," I said, tears springing to my eyes. It was awful to see her like that, so undone. "I'll go after the internship, before school starts. You can make whatever arrangements you want. Don't worry, Mom. I'll do it."

"Thank you," she breathed. "Thanks."

"Don't mention it," I murmured, sliding my hand into the pocket of my raincoat to feel the smooth surface of the cherrywood compass case I had deposited there earlier that day. It seemed to give off a faint heat on this drab, sad day, although that, of course, was impossible. There goes my summer vacation, I thought, and if I know my cousin (and I did know my cousin), there goes my sanity as well.

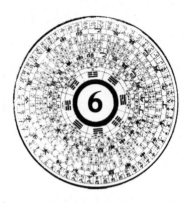

I was sitting at my workstation on the twenty-third floor of the green glass CanBoard office tower, leaning back in my swivel chair and gazing out the window at the faint outline of mountains in the distance. Power views don't come a whole lot better than the one from the west-facing windows of the interns' office: the steep, jagged, snowcapped peaks of the Canadian Rockies, as seen from an upper story of a building so large that it takes up an entire city block of downtown Calgary, and so high that it dominates the skyline.

It was a few minutes past seven-thirty on the last night of my internship. I had just cleaned out my desk. There had been a little party for the interns an hour earlier. After cupcakes and fruit punch and balloons, the others had said their good-byes and left for the airport to catch planes to Toronto and Winnipeg and Montreal.

I stayed behind. My plane wasn't out until the morning and, besides, I wanted to soak up the atmosphere, to bask in the knowledge that, for the moment at least, I was living out my dream. I, Miranda Liu, was well on my way to having a small part to play in transforming the world as we know it.

Yes!

It was a heady feeling and I wanted to enjoy it while I could. Live, drink, and be merry, I thought, helping myself to yet another cupcake (gooey chocolate with pink icing), for tomorrow . . . tomorrow I go to Moose Jaw. Well, Moose Jaw via Regina, the capital of Saskatchewan.

The thought punctured my good mood like a nail flattening a tire. I deflated, which was fairly remarkable given the number of cupcakes I had eaten.

Mom had made all the arrangements, booking my plane ticket and a hotel and a rental car. She had called to give me confirmation numbers.

"But I can't drive!"

"Brian will drive."

So, yes, Brian was coming. I rolled my eyes in exasperation. I was supposed to meet up with Doofus at the Regina Airport; his plane from Vancouver was due forty minutes after mine from Calgary. Then we would drive the rental car from Regina to Moose Jaw.

"What about you?" I'd pleaded. "Aren't you coming?"

Because technically Brian and I were both minors. Surely she wasn't supposed to let us go roaming around Saskatchewan without adult supervision.

But no. "I have to take care of Dad and Liam." Which was true, I suppose. Both of them were super-dependent on her for pretty much everything. Besides, flying made her symptoms a lot worse. Made her even more tired. Still.

"You haven't headed out yet?"

My heart did a little bump, before I registered the voice as both familiar and friendly. I swiveled my chair around to see Thierry Maille from Channel Development. Thierry was a Quebecer in his mid-twenties, small and wiry, with stand-up tufts of orange and blue hair – retro punk in its latest incarnation. Most of CanBoard's employees were young, some only half a dozen years older than me, making my dream of working for the consortium in the near future not as unattainable as you might think, particularly given my test scores in Mediated Reality markup language and Web Metadata.

"Just hanging out," I said. "My plane isn't out until tomorrow." Truth was, I didn't really relish the thought of going back to the dorm now that everyone had taken off. Although I hadn't managed to make real friends with any of my fellow interns – the pace wouldn't have allowed for much socializing, even if I had been more outgoing – the prospect of empty rooms and silent halls made me feel a bit bummed, and a little lost. I had the feeling that I would rattle around. I hate that feeling.

"What's that?" Thierry had spotted the cherrywood box containing the *lo p'an*. It was on top of the stuff I had removed from the desk and piled up in a bin for transport back to the dorm.

"It's something my grandmother gave me. Pretty cool." I unlatched the box, removed the compass from the case, and handed it to him.

"Wow! This is one of those *feng shui* things, isn't it?"

"It's what you call a *lo p'an*, a geomancer's compass."

He turned it over in his hand, tracing the concentric rings with his finger, peering at the Chinese characters. "What a beauty. How old is it, do you know?"

"I do," I said, feeling a little tickle of pride. "Seventeenth century. But how do you know about this stuff? *Feng shui*, I mean."

"My wife's into it. She took a workshop."

"Really? A workshop?" I remembered my conversation with A-Ma; how *feng shui* had to do with grave sites and stuff like that. "What sort of things did she learn?"

Thierry laughed. "Well, for starters, she learned that wealth escapes through open toilets, so now we have to keep the toilet lids down. My dog still doesn't know what hit him."

That rang a bell. When my cousin Oliver was little, he used to lope, whooping, through the house, going from bathroom to bathroom (and the Pender Street house had six of them) on this weird kind of mission he had set himself to raise all lowered toilet lids. Who knows what he was thinking? Maybe it was his idea of fun. This drove the grown-ups wild – A-Ma had insisted, *insisted*, that toilet seats must be down at all times (well, except when you were using them) – so off Brian would be dispatched, to close the lids Oliver had opened. And around and around they'd go, making everybody dizzy and cranky. I laughed and shook my head. What a crazy memory. "It was an article of faith in my family that the only reason we didn't go under during the Wall Street Meltdown of '08 was that we kept our toilet lids down," I told Thierry. "I never realized that was *feng shui*."

"Of course, there's other stuff besides the toilet lids," he said. "Stuff about mirror placement and the orientation of your bedroom and where you should have plants and where you shouldn't. . . . You do know there's a *feng shui* network on WorldBoard?"

"I didn't."

Well, it made sense. The last few years had seen an explosion of WebTV channels. There were cooking channels and sports channels and craft channels and cartoon channels. You name it. The difference between cable TV and WebTV channels had to do with the experience, of course – people turned on Window Walls to watch programs, while they logged onto WebTV to take part in activities through virtual reality.

"Yep. We launched it a few months ago," Thierry replied. "Just dial into the New Age portal and key in 'feng shui' if you want to check it out." He handed me back the compass. "Quite the artifact, Miranda. You'll let me know if you ever want to sell it? Present for the wife. Can't be too many of these around."

I laughed. "No chance of that. It's been in my family for a zillion years. You know how people say, 'If I did that, my grandmother would turn over in her grave'? Well, Chinese don't just turn over in their graves. According to my grandmother, they turn into horrible monsters and come after you."

"Well, if you ever change your mind," he said. "You've got a little chocolate . . ." He pointed to the right corner of his mouth.

Hurriedly I dabbed at my face with a crumpled party napkin.

"Got it," he said. "I'm off now. Best of luck. I won't say good-bye. I have a feeling you'll be back here before too long."

I beamed. "I hope so." Then my heart sank. First I had to go to Moose Jaw.

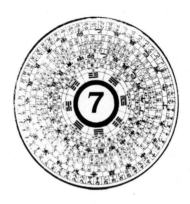

After Thierry left, I swiveled back to face the window. I was about to put the *lo p'an* back in its box when it occurred to me that I'd never actually stopped and taken a good long look at the compass. Whatever I might think of its usefulness as a tool, it was, at the very least, beautiful and exotic. I counted the ivory rings surrounding the *yin-yang* symbol at the compass's center – one, two, three . . . eighteen in all. Whatever that signified. And it had to signify something. For old-school Chinese, it's all about the numbers – two means this and six means that. Then there are the lucky numbers and the unlucky numbers, and the *really* unlucky numbers . . . don't get me started. As for what those Chinese characters inscribed on the rings meant . . . not a clue. They looked like so many chicken scratches to me.

I closed my eyes, leaned back in my chair, and let my

fingers drift over the bumpy surface of the compass. A pop-up of Sebastian's face as I had last seen it appeared in my mind's eye. Summoned home from blind kids' camp for A-Ma's funeral, he had described to me how he was trying to master Braille before his eyesight completely failed. Blind by age thirteen. How would it be to have sight and to lose it, to know what you were missing? It made me sad. It pissed me off.

Feeling grim, I replaced the *lo p'an* in its case but didn't close the lid. Instead I picked up my enviro-mote and used it to close the miniblinds and power up my computer. I logged onto the New Age portal and keyed in "feng shui." When the screen popped up, I did a search for "geomancer's compass." Listed among the options was a virtual tour. I clicked on it, ticked the payment box – which let my bank access my account to pay the provider – and downloaded the tour onto a card, which I inserted in my I-spex. (One of the perks of interning for CanBoard was that WorldBoard was in the middle of beta testing I-spex. You wear them like eyeglasses instead of having a big clunky head-mounted display, or HMD, wrapped around your noggin – much lighter than HMDs and they don't make you look like an alien, which is always a plus. Eventually everyone will have a brain implant, of course, but that's a ways off.)

I put on the spectacles and pressed the power button on the right earpiece.

Whoa, I thought. Pass me a barf bag.

There was the usual sense of dislocation and head spin you always experience when being bumped into a virtual environment, and then there I was, all gnarly and queased out, standing in what appeared to be a cavernous room at the center of a large 3-D circular structure. The only illumination came from a spotlight that dangled high over my head. The pale, silvery light it cast extended just beyond the edge of the structure, then pixilated out into blackness. I looked down to find myself standing on a medallion consisting of a black-and-white *yin-yang* symbol. It appeared far down, farther than it should have, given my small size – that's typical of VR, the impression that you've suddenly shot up a foot in height. I pirouetted slowly – no point in moving quickly; that would only make me dizzier and contribute to the not great feeling that I was going to spew any second. Why had I eaten all those cupcakes? The *yin-yang* symbol was composed of tiny black and white squares, like the tiles in a mosaic. It was about four feet across. Around this central medallion spun concentric circles made of some kind of metal, possibly brass, one after the other. I squatted carefully and ran my hand over the surface of the circle closest to the center. Like the compass, it was densely covered with writing; thankfully, this writing was in English. I dropped to my hands and knees and peered closer. "Fire, earth, lake, heaven . . ." I read haltingly, crawling in a clockwise direction.

"South, southwest, west, northwest . . ." A voice from beyond the circle of light.

I stiffened and glanced sharply up. Too sharply: head-spin. "What?" I croaked, my gorge wobbling about in my midsection in a way I didn't trust.

"That is the Later Heaven Circle you are reading," the voice continued. "It is the vehicle of divination and represents change and movement." The voice sounded like it belonged to an old man who spoke fluent English, but with a definite Chinese accent.

I pressed my fingers to my temples and closed my eyes, trying to slow the tilted ring-around-the-rosy going on in my brain. "What are you?" I managed to say. "Are you a disembodied voice or an avatar?"

"An avatar," replied the voice. "In the original sense of the word."

I sat back on my haunches and opened my eyes slowly. Easy does it – that was the trick. "What?"

"A variant version of a continuing basic entity," replied the voice. "*Merriam-Webster's Collegiate Dictionary*." And with that the avatar floated forward from the blackness. Like most such animations, it was featureless, but its creator had taken the time to characterize it with an old man's stoop and shuffle. It held a cane in its right hand. The handle was a glowing green globe.

I frowned. "You look familiar somehow. Do I know you?"

"You do!" The avatar chuckled. It placed the tip of the cane on the first concentric circle, which was about the same height as a stair riser, and hoisted itself onto the compass. Folding its hands over its stomach, it rocked tentatively back and forth on its heels, humming softly.

I recognized the posture instantly. "The Grandfather?"

"Indeed," it replied. "I've been expecting you."

I stared, unable to believe my eyes.

"Aren't you going to say something?" it asked. "After all, it's been three years."

"Three years since you *died*."

"Yes, and . . . ?"

"Well, that's the point, isn't it?" I asked. "You're dead. That means you're no longer real."

"That depends on what reality you inhabit," replied The Grandfather. "Where do you think people go when they die, Miranda?"

"Heaven . . . hell," I said. "To tell the truth, I never thought cyberspace was an option."

"There are worlds between worlds. This right now . . . where we are now . . . happens to be one of those worlds."

"But don't you belong in . . . I don't know . . . some Buddhist heaven or other? I mean, you were such a big deal. In life, that is."

"There is no Buddhist heaven," it replied. "There are the Six Realms. And, not to put too fine a point on it, I am stuck between realms at present, and will be until we can solve the problem of my brother's disappearance."

I was so not satisfied. "Right. Stuck. Yet you somehow managed to get yourself encoded into a virtual reality tour?"

The avatar nodded. "So I could communicate with you."

That sounded pretty out there. "How do I know you're not some artificial intelligence entity modeled on The Grandfather?"

"Why would you think that?"

"The way you talk, for one. Your English. The Grandfather sounded like he'd just got off the boat from Shanghai."

The avatar shrugged. "An upgrade. Just a matter of installing a dictionary. But let's get on with it. We really don't have much time. Did you know that your cousin Aubrey is due for a massive heart attack in two weeks? It seems that her potassium levels are dangerously low."

It was like it had reached into my body and squeezed my heart in its hand, like my heart was caught in some kind of vise; for a moment I could barely breathe. Poor Aubrey. I could only dimly remember the cute, bouncy teenager she had been, a little plump maybe, but never fat. "Stop it. How can you joke about something like that?"

"Oh, I'm not joking, Miranda," the avatar replied. "This will most certainly happen if we have not rectified the situation in two weeks' time."

"But how do you know? How can you possibly know?"

"We have our ways."

"We? Who's 'we'?"

"The *feng shui* channel, of course. It's more than just a way to distribute content, you know. Much more. Oh, and did you know you are scheduled to be eaten by a shark within the next twenty-four months?"

"*What?*"

"Off the coast of Bermuda."

"I didn't know I was going to Bermuda."

"Surprise."

"Oh, man." I was starting to quease again – all those cupcakes doing their cupcake dance in my stomach. Eaten by a shark? "What you're talking about is in the future," I protested. "How can you possibly know what's going to happen in the future?"

"There is no future, Miranda. There is no past. Now is all there is. The present moment."

"Maybe for you . . . because you're *dead*!"

The avatar sighed. "For you too. For all sentient beings. You just don't realize it." It shook its head. "I'd forgotten how contrary you can be."

"I have an inquiring mind."

"All well and good, but we need to focus. Can you focus?"

A shark? *Really?* "I can focus."

"Well, do. Now, what do you know about our problem? What did your grandmother tell you?"

"She told me that I was in charge of the *lo p'an*, but she didn't tell me how to use it and, honestly, I don't read Chinese –"

The avatar interrupted me mid-sentence. Its tone was withering. "Mastering an instrument as complex as the *lo p'an* requires much more than the ability to read Chinese. A good geomancer will have some innate talent, but he must also apprentice himself to a master and study for many years before his readings will be accurate. Of course your grandmother did not *tell* you how to use it. She did not know how to use it, and neither will you. It is *I* who will use it."

"So how come I have it?"

"Isn't it obvious?" asked the avatar. "Because I am a digital entity. The *lo p'an* is real. Digital entities cannot carry actual objects."

"So I'm a *lo p'an* mule?"

"Essentially."

This came as both a relief and an affront. I snorted. So much for my big important mission, so much for me being The Chosen One.

"And a Seeker."

"Pardon?"

"A Seeker," the avatar repeated. "That's you."

I should have known. Classic avatar speak. You're not a player; you're a Seeker. It's not a game; it's a Quest. You don't win or lose; you Triumph or are Utterly Destroyed. That sort of thing. It was just something about being an avatar; if they had DNA, which they don't, the impulse to indulge in avatar speak would be in their DNA. "What do you mean, Seeker?"

"One who seeks Qianfu."

I sighed. "I hate to break this to you, but this is not going to be as easy as you and A-Ma seem to think. Over a hundred years have gone by. Anyone who knew anything about what happened to Qianfu's bones is long dead."

"There are records," the avatar said. "Databases –"

"Hello," I interrupted. "Which databases?"

"All relevant ones."

"Databases are only as useful as their data," I countered, "and in case you didn't know, unmarked graves tend not to be in databases. That's why they call them unmarked."

"Oh, you'd be surprised at what ends up in a database." The avatar's tone turned breezy. "But you downloaded a virtual tour of the *lo p'an*, Miranda. Don't you want to take it?"

"I guess," I said. "Wait a minute. How did you know I was going to download this tour? I didn't even know there was a *feng shui* channel before tonight."

"We have our ways," replied the avatar. "Now." Stepping back and turning slightly away from me, it extended its arms out wide. "What we appear to be standing on is a 3-D model of a geomancer's compass, much enlarged. An ordinary compass aligns with the magnetic pole to determine directions or bearings in the physical realm. A geomancer's compass, on the other hand, is used to select a place to live, in agricultural planning, and to align the dead. The idea is to use the laws of heaven and earth to maximize *chi*. Do you follow me?"

"Sort of," I muttered. "You know this is all bogus, don't you? Utter hooey."

"I most certainly do not," it said crisply. "There are other differences between a *lo p'an* and an ordinary compass." It pointed to the words carved into the concentric rings. "Take these *feng shui* formulas embedded on the Heaven Dial, for example. You won't find these on an ordinary compass."

"Formulas for what?"

"Various things." It began pointing out the different formulas. "This one has to do with the eight main life aspirations. That one there, Flying Stars, that's a time and space system. And this . . . this formula focuses on the interaction between a particular element – water, wood, fire, earth, or metal – ruling the front door of a building and the elements ruling the birth dates of its occupants."

Suddenly, as if a switch had been thrown on, the metal surface on which we were standing began to rotate slowly in a clockwise direction, like a merry-go-round. I staggered a little, then struggled to regain my balance, not easy in a virtual environment. "What's going on?"

"We are standing on the Heaven Dial. Underneath this dial is the Earth Plate. The Heaven Dial rotates freely on the Earth Plate. Look out!"

I jumped just in time to miss tripping over a taut red velvet rope that stretched from one side of the compass to the other, eight inches above the surface. "What's that?"

"That's the Heaven Center Cross Line. It crosses the Earth Plate and Heaven Dial at a ninety-degree angle."

The compass was picking up speed.

"Can you stop this thing?" I complained. "I'm dizzy." I sank down onto my knees, then pitched forward onto my hands.

"I'm trying to demonstrate how the *lo p'an* works," the avatar objected.

"And I'm about to heave chocolate cupcakes and fruit punch all over your precious compass!"

The avatar sighed. "All right." It hoisted its cane into the air. There was a clicking sound and the compass slowed, then lurched to a grinding stop.

I rolled over onto my back and laid my hands over my forehead. Both were clammy. My heart was racing and my stomach was a swamp with attitude. "Remember, I've got I-spex on," I gasped. "CanBoard hasn't worked out the registration error yet. Balance is an issue."

"Now I remember," said the avatar. "You were the one with the weak stomach."

It was true. Most children's parties when I was a kid ended up with me in the bathroom heaving up cake, and no car trip or airplane flight was complete without its upchucks. On the plus side, my dodgy stomach made it possible for me to focus on my studies without the usual socially generated, alcohol-fueled events that were beginning to distract many of my peers. A mixed blessing, I guess you'd say.

"I seem to remember you throwing up on me once, didn't you?" noted the avatar.

I flushed. "When I was like *five*."

"On my birthday. If I'm not mistaken, you managed to hit the cake as well. That was memorable."

"You were jiggling me on your knee," I retorted. "I had candy coming out my ears. What did you expect?" I rolled carefully onto my left side and slowly up to a seated position. Then I got onto my hands and knees, steadying myself before standing gingerly, adjusting my I-spex, and taking deep breaths in an attempt to settle my stomach.

"Are you all right?"

"Yes. Just, let's take things easy, OK? No spinning and jumping."

The avatar seemed disappointed. "That animation took hours."

"Well, sorry, but I'm not an avatar and I'm not dead. I have a stomach and a head and, right now, neither of them can handle the round-and-round-we-go part."

"If you insist. Now, where was I?"

"Oh, I don't know," I said vaguely. "Dials, plates . . ."

"Rings," said the avatar. "There are eighteen of them in this particular compass – it varies – but only three are critical to our enterprise. Now, listen up, Miranda. They are the Twenty-Four Directions Circle, the Earlier Heaven Circle, and the Later Heaven Circle . . ."

Boring!

"This one is the Twenty-Four Directions Circle; it describes the realm of the earth and the energy that flows in it. This is the Earlier Heaven Circle; it describes the realm of the underlying permanence of the Tao, the principles or laws of existence that do not change. And this one –"

I held up my hand. "Hold on. You lost me. I don't have a clue what you're talking about. Grandfather? *Grandfather?*" My field of vision had begun to crackle with dropouts, and the audio was fading in and out. My I-spex were losing their charge. "You're cutting out," I said, as my eye screens went black.

"Being eaten by a shark is a painful death," I heard the avatar say in a faint voice, as if its owner was tumbling down a well away from me. "That's what they say-ay-ay-ay-ay."

And there it was – the void. Nothing for my senses to grapple with – no color, no sound or sense of touch. I told myself that I was not floundering in nothingness, which was what it felt like, but suspended in a kind of air lock between reality and virtual reality. Even now, after years of operating in VR environments, a kind of terror wells up in me – the brain finds a sudden lack of sensation difficult to reconcile with conscious thought, and it panics. This happens to everyone, I told myself, just hold on and it will be over.

Then there was a click and the dead hum of the empty channel. All I could say was, thank the Celestial Worthy of Numinous Treasure.

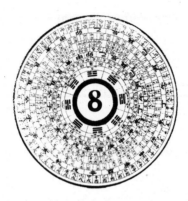

I peeled off my I-spex and squeezed my eyes shut. I rubbed them hard, then opened them. When I had logged onto the virtual tour, I had been seated at my workstation. Now I stood in the approximate center of the large open area assigned to interns during the summer. Darkness had begun to seep into the big room; all that was left of the flaming sunset was a coral-edged horizon. I checked my watch. It was going on nine o'clock. Then my phone rang. Without checking the call display, I answered it. And instantly regretted it. It was Brian. *Groan.*

"Randi," he greeted me. "Cuz."

I winced. I hated being called Randi and he knew it. "Hi, Bri," I countered. Problem was, he didn't mind being called Bri. In fact, he kind of liked it.

"Long time, no hear." Why did he always sound so cheerful? It was massively irritating.

"What do you mean? I saw you at A-Ma's funeral."

"Seeing is not hanging out with."

I was glad the webcam was turned off, so he couldn't see my face go scarlet. He was right, of course. I had made a point of avoiding him at the funeral. It would have been too weird hanging out with him and not saying anything about what A-Ma had told me, all the while knowing that we would be going on this fool's errand to Moose Jaw in a couple of weeks.

"Yeah, well," I said, "I had a lot on my mind."

"I guess there's not much we have in common, now that you're like a one-woman brain trust and I'm an illiterate gardener."

"Hey, you're a dyslexic *bonsai* master, not an illiterate gardener," I corrected him. "There's a difference."

"No there isn't." He was joking and he wasn't. Brian had always been supersensitive about being dyslexic. How not? The Chinese-Canadian community placed an insanely strong emphasis on education; most of the kids we grew up with would go on to become professionals – lawyers, doctors, scientists, or accountants. Not Brian. So understandably he had a bit of a self-esteem issue, which would have made me feel sorry for him if his relentless cheerfulness hadn't annoyed me so much. Brian needed to take a few sadness lessons. Seriously. He was way too enthusiastic about everything. "But that's not what I'm calling about," he continued. "I'm calling about this romantic trip for two that you and your pathetic loser cousin – now, who would that be? Oh yes, that would be me – are supposedly taking to Moose Jaw. Like, tomorrow."

"What? Did Mom just tell you?"

"Tonight. An hour ago. You mean you've known about this all along?"

I remembered back to A-Ma's funeral, when I had asked Mom if Brian knew about the "family curse" and our "mission," and she had said, "Not yet. You know how he is, Miranda. We thought it best to wait." She had waited, all right.

"Yeah, well, since just before A-Ma died. And it's not a romantic trip. It's just . . . a trip."

"Whew," joked Brian, "that's a relief. I am your first cousin, after all. A romantic trip would be a little awkward."

"Don't be disgusting."

"Not that you're not perfectly attractive. If you like freakishly small nerd girls."

"Shut up."

"Shut up, yourself. No, on second thought, don't shut up. Tell me why we're going to Moose Jaw."

How much did he know? Anything? "What did Mom tell you?"

"*Nada, niente, rien.* In case you don't know, that's Spanish, Italian, and French for 'nothing.' She said you'd fill me in. So fill me in."

Nothing? I'd fill him in? I had to explain this wacked scheme to Brian myself? Nice work, Mom!

"I'll tell you tomorrow."

"What? Randi, no. Tell me now."

"When we meet up in Regina. And don't call me Randi."

"Now you're making me really curious."

"Tomorrow."

"No no no no no, Randi. Come on. Please. Tell me. I'm going to die of curiosity."

"No, you're not." I hung up. Two seconds later, my cell rang. I checked caller ID. Of course it was Brian. I turned the ringer off. I couldn't deal with him tonight; it would be bad enough tomorrow.

The virtual tour had left me with ringing ears and a headache. I closed my eyes and massaged my temples. Brian was so going to need to be managed. The prospect exhausted me.

I went onto the net, keyed in the words "Moose Jaw," and downloaded as much geo-coded data on the town and its environs as I could fit onto my flash drive – land registry, infrastructure data, information on landfill, the Global Subterranean Survey, and general Geographic Information System stuff. I logged off, strapped on my Zypad – a touch screen computer on an armband – and liberated an extra pair of I-spex from the storage room. Each intern had received one complimentary set, so technically I was stealing the extra set, but I knew they had a huge number of them in inventory. One set wouldn't be missed. Then I turned off my desk lamp and, picking my way through the whirring clean-o-bots that overran the glassy tower at sunset, headed for the elevator and the empty dorm.

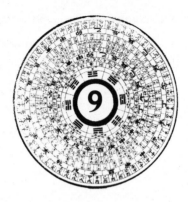

We spotted it from miles away. It was hard not to, given its ginormity and the fact that the farmland on either side of the Trans-Canada between Regina and Moose Jaw is flatter than flat, the very definition of flat – I mean, if you grew up in Saskatchewan, you could be forgiven for thinking that the world was flat because, really, why would it ever occur to you that it wasn't?

"What the . . . ?" Brian squinted bug-eyed into the distance through a pair of retro Ray-Bans. He was driving the lavender Heibao Helio that Mom had rented for us at the Regina Airport. It was one of the new plug-in hybrids that came with mandatory cruise control, which meant that, as hyper as Brian got, he could only ever do the speed limit. This was good because Brian has that irritatingly adolescent male need-for-speed gene in spades, and I really didn't want to be a passenger in anything that gave him the option of putting the pedal to the metal.

"It looks . . . like a moose," I speculated. A moment later, the GPS, whose name was Hermione, confirmed this in her ritzy Bond girl British accent. "On your left is Mac the Moose, the world's largest moose statue, completed in 1984. Mac is made of metal piping, mesh, and cement. He stands thirty-two feet tall and weighs ten tons."

"A giant moose statue," said Brian. "That's something you don't see every day!"

To which Hermione added, "Mac the Moose serves as the gateway to the city of Moose Jaw, Saskatchewan."

"Oh, gateway," said Brian. He nodded sagely. "In China the gateways are guarded by lions; in Moose Jaw, by moose." He elbowed me across the divide. "Hear that, cuz? Almost there. We've been driving for forty minutes and I still haven't been able to wring the reason we're going to Moose Jaw out of you."

I sighed. You need to time-release information to Brian in manageable gobbets. Otherwise his brain explodes. "I did so tell you," I said. "A-Ma wanted us to pay homage to The Grandfather's brother at his grave site – you know, Qingming stuff." Qingming Festival, a.k.a. Bright Festival, a.k.a. Tomb Sweeping Day, is when you drag the whole family out to the cemetery and perform prayers and ceremonies and rituals in honor of your ancestors so they won't be pissed off at you and wreck your life. You also tidy up the grave and put fresh flowers out and set off firecrackers to ward off evil spirits. "I guess his grave, being out in Moose Jaw and all, hadn't been swept for a long time and it was . . . I don't know . . . preying on her conscience. She was, like, stressing out about it. Anyway, it was A-Ma's dying wish and that's why we're here." I wasn't exactly lying. I'm sure A-Ma would have wanted us to sweep Qianfu's tomb . . . once we found it.

"*C'mon.* There's got to be more to it than that. And what was The Grandfather's brother doing out in Moose Jaw in the first place?"

"People don't always stay in the same place," I said vaguely.

"Turn right in half a mile." This from Hermione.

Brian turned off the Trans-Canada onto Caribou Street. "Sure you don't want some chips? They're righteous."

"They're disgusting and very bad for you." I glared at him as disapprovingly as a person who had consumed her body weight in cupcakes the night before could manage. Brian eats constantly. He had been eating when I met him at the arrivals gate in the airport and he was still eating. His backpack bulged with snacks, none of them healthy. So did the gazillion pockets of the khaki photographer's vest he wore over an orange and peacock blue Hawaiian shirt featuring what looked like exploding palm trees. By rights he should have been the size of an elephant, but his hyperactivity coupled with his height (he was nearly six feet tall to my five) kept his weight in check.

"In one quarter mile, turn right onto Main Street," Hermione crooned.

Brian turned onto Moose Jaw's wide Main Street, four lanes separated by a brick median brimming with flowers and lined, for the most part, with heritage buildings dating from 1900 to the late 1920s – Italianate in style, constructed in stone or brick or faced with limestone. He was impressed. "Look at this architecture. I didn't expect this."

"What did you expect?"

"I don't know . . . early grain elevator?"

"Your destination is on the right," Hermione advised.

And there it was, the hotel Mom had booked for us, the Prairie Rose, an unprepossessing four-story walk-up built in the 1920s, drab and water stained.

"Now, that," said Brian, "*that* is early grain elevator."

I felt a tug of anxiety. What had Mom been thinking? It had looked so much better in the online photos. Would the bathroom be clean? What about bugs? Have I mentioned that I am just the teensiest bit germaphobic? I patted my knapsack. Relief at having brought along a travel pack of industrial-strength hand wipes washed over me.

"More prairie than rose, I think," said Brian. "Well, it's not as if we're going to be spending much time here. Or are we? Just what are we doing in this burg, Randi?"

I was beginning to feel a little shaky: hypoglycemia alert. The car smelled oppressively of potato chip; it was late morning, hot and stuffy, and in penance for last night's cupcake orgy, I had skipped breakfast. "Just leave it alone for a few minutes, OK? Let's check into this dump and get something to eat, and I promise I'll give you the full scoop."

10

"Yessir, the Prairie Rose, she's full of history, all right," the desk clerk informed us as we checked in. A wizened old prune of a man in a tartan vest, he fit right in with the hotel lobby's threadbare carpet and water stained ceiling. His teeth were yellow and kind of crumbly and his fingers were stained with nicotine. Also, he had this really nasty wart on his chin with stiff white hairs sprouting out of it. His tarnished nameplate identified him as Oscar. When I think of Oscar, I think of two things: Oscar the Grouch on that old television show and the Oscar Mayer wiener. I wouldn't like anyone to associate a grouch or a wiener with my name. What was his mother thinking?

"History?" asked Brian. "How so?" Brian likes to talk to people. Anybody. Creepy, not creepy—doesn't matter. Especially homeless people, whom I avoid like the plague because they're usually pretty dirty. I know it's not their fault, but still.

"Oh, we've had us some pretty famous clientele over the years," Oscar said proudly. He spoke with what I was beginning to suspect might be an actual Saskatchewan accent, pinched and nasal, with a peculiar hint of Irish to it. "Why, Al Capone used to stay here when he was in town."

I wrinkled my nose. The lobby smelled funny, like a combination of mouse pee and mold. Or maybe it was Oscar. Whatever it was didn't bode well for my allergies. "Al Capone?" The name sounded vaguely familiar, but not so much that I could place it.

Brian turned to face me. "Randi. C'mon! You've never heard of Al Capone? The famous gangster? You know, *Scarface*?"

"I was never much for rap music."

Brian sighed and shook his head. "Not *those* gangsters, Randi. The *real* gangsters – back in the early twentieth century." He turned back to Oscar. "When was Capone here?"

Happy to have found an audience, Oscar leaned forward conspiratorially. "In the 1920s. During Prohibition. You see, the Canadian Pacific's Soo Line runs from Chicago to Moose Jaw. That's how the Mob moved liquor across the border into the U.S. They'd hide the hooch in the tunnels – in those days, they called them the Boozarium – until it was time for a shipment, then carry it out through a tunnel that opened into a shed in the CPR rail yard, load it onto the train, and send it south to speakeasies run by the Mob. Just like that, bold as brass."

Hooch? Boozarium? Maybe I should have consulted the Urban Dictionary. But I did know who the Mob was.

I could see that Brian was enthralled. His eyes sparkled and he leaned in closer to Oscar, doubtless breathing potato chip breath all over him. Oscar didn't seem to mind. He was probably breathing cigarette breath right back at him. "Tunnels?" Brian asked. "What tunnels?" I suppressed a sigh and rolled my eyes. Brian loved all things underground: sewers, caves, the Chunnel . . .

"You don't know about the tunnels?" Oscar sounded surprised. "Why, the Moose Jaw tunnels are world famous. Run all under downtown, crisscrossed and interconnected. Went on forever; nobody knows how many miles long they might have been in their heyday. Over the years many of them were filled in. New construction. Infill."

"Brian, come on," I urged him, tugging at the hem of his photographer's vest. "Can we hurry this along a little? I have to pee."

Brian grinned and pointed at me. "Princess Tiny Bladder," he told Oscar. "That's what we call her at home. Hold on, Randi. This'll only take a minute. The tunnels, Oscar – did the gangsters actually build them?"

I scowled, pressing my legs together. I really did have to pee.

"Nope," said Oscar. "Steam tunnels originally."

"Steam tunnels?" Brian's appetite for long, detailed explanations was one that I didn't share, maybe because I could read about what interested me and he couldn't. If there was one thing I knew, it was that once Brian latched onto a source of information you couldn't beat him off it with a two-by-four. He just glommed onto whatever it was and wouldn't let go. Like a Jack Russell terrier, like a pit bull with good intentions. We might be here for a while. I sighed and began casting my eyes around the lobby in search of a public toilet.

"Around 1900 all the buildings in Moose Jaw were heated by steam," Oscar was explaining. "That meant everybody had a coal-fueled boiler in the basement. Now, I don't know if you're familiar with boilers, sonny . . ."

"Excuse me," I murmured, "but is that . . . ?" I pointed to a door with faded lettering on it that I thought might have, in the distant past, read "Restroom."

Oscar nodded but did not break stride. "If you got you a boiler in your basement, you want to keep an eye on it at all times. Your boiler, you don't know what it might do. It might rupture, the seams can split, tubes can collapse or dislodge and spray scalding hot steam and smoke out of the air intake and firing chute . . . and you don't even want to think about what can happen if one boils dry."

I crossed the lobby to the door, extracted a tissue from my pocket, and used it to open the restroom door. Germs have been known to live over two hours on doorknobs.

"When it's forty-below, you don't want to be coming up from one basement and out into the cold, just to go across the street or next door so you can go down into a second basement," Oscar was explaining. "By developing a system of tunnels that opened onto *all* the basements in this area, starting at the train station, the boiler men could move from basement to basement without coming upstairs. And the women liked it better because the men weren't constantly tracking snow and mud in from the streets."

The restroom was a one-seater and it wasn't pretty. Cracked linoleum floor, a stained sink with no stopper, a wavy mirror smudged with fingerprints, and a toilet I didn't trust for a minute. Unrolling a length of toilet paper, I carefully lined the seat with it, making sure I didn't touch the plastic. (For those of you who think it's totally germaphobic to line a public toilet seat with paper before dropping your bare bum onto it, I have two words for you: fecal bacteria.)

"Does this hotel have a door leading into one of the tunnels?" I heard Brian ask. The walls were very thin.

"Yep," Oscar replied. "All the basements in this area from this period do. We keep it locked because of the tours. Wouldn't want tourists wandering off and ending up in our basement by mistake. Though, come to think of it, it might be good for business."

"There are *tours*?" Brian sounded excited.

I peed and wiped myself, then turned and began to peel the paper off the seat.

"Sure are," Oscar replied. "Let me see if I can find the brochure."

I wrapped some toilet paper around my hand so that I wouldn't have to touch either the toilet lid or the handle, lowered the lid, and flushed. I washed my hands and reemerged to see Oscar handing Brian a dog-eared brochure.

"Thanks, man." Brian folded the brochure in half and shoved it into one of his many vest pockets. He would need me to read it. "Randi," he greeted me. "You didn't fall in."

"Brian," I warned him. Honestly. You couldn't go to the bathroom without him announcing it to the world. I crossed the lobby to the desk.

"Mrs. Liu?" Oscar consulted a piece of paper. "You'll be wanting the two rooms? Not the one?"

I blushed. Mrs. Liu? He thought Brian and I were married. Gross. "Miss Liu," I corrected him. "It's Miss, not Mrs."

"I'm sorry." He perched a pair of wire-rimmed spectacles halfway down his nose and peered at the piece of paper. "The reservation was made by a Mrs. Daisy Liu."

"That's my mother," I explained. "And yes, we definitely want two rooms."

Brian laughed – a long, embarrassing hee-haw – and slapped his thigh. He waggled his finger at Oscar. "Not what you're thinking," he told him. "In the first place, we're just sweet sixteen. In the second place, we're cousins, and definitely *not* the kissing kind."

"I thought you two looked kind of young to be married," mused Oscar. "But I never can tell with your people. Old, young, whatever . . . you all look kind of the same to me. Could you sign this?" He handed Brian a form; Brian pushed it over the counter to me. While I was signing it, Oscar handed Brian two keys – not key cards, actual keys. "Rooms 14 and 15. Third floor. There's an elevator through those doors. You enjoy your stay now." He chuckled. "And don't worry if you hear some strange noises while you're here. The way the wind blows across the prairie sometimes makes our old plumbing howl like a ghost in a bottle."

"We 'all look kind of the same'?" I hissed to Brian, as he toted our luggage to a small mirrored elevator flanked by two desperate-looking palms. "Was that racist or what?"

"Take it easy, cuz," said Brian. "Poor old Oscar isn't a racist. He's just easily confused. How about we grab some lunch once we've dumped the luggage? Then we can suss out the tunnel tours."

"This isn't a vacation, you know. We have work to do." I peered at the elevator button with distrust. "Would you . . . ?" I gestured toward the button.

He shook his head. "You and germs." He pressed the button. "Don't you want to see where Al Capone hung out?"

"Uh . . . no. Why would I?"

"Why would you do anything? Because it's fun and interesting. But I forget, you don't like fun."

"I like fun."

"Oh, sure you do. 'Fun-loving.' 'A barrel of fun.' That's the way I describe you to people."

"You talk about me to people?"

"Of course I do. You're my cousin."

That pulled me up short. I rarely talked about Brian; in fact, I rarely talked about any member of my family. Why was that? Because I found the subject depressing? Because, if people knew the truth, they might think there was something wrong with me too?

The elevator door shuddered open. We stepped inside and Brian stabbed the button for the third floor. The elevator lurched its way up and the door creaked open. It sounded like a tomb creaking open, or what I imagined a tomb creaking open would sound like. I had never actually heard one and hoped I never would. Wherever Qianfu was buried, I sure as hell hoped it wasn't a tomb. I stepped out into a narrow, sloped hall flanked by numbered doors, with Brian on my heels, begging, "Can we go to the tunnels? Please? Please?"

I pointed at the door to room 14. "Unlock, please."

"Randi, it's just a key."

"You don't know where that key's been."

"Where would it have been? It's a key."

"Just do it."

Brian grinned. "Oh, now I get it, Miss Germaphobe. You've brought me along to do all your dirty work for you: pressing buttons, unlocking doors . . . I hope you don't expect me to flush your toilet for you."

I shook my head. "True germaphobes wash their hands compulsively and avoid contact with all surfaces. I wash my hands as needed and only avoid contact with surfaces that might be contaminated. I'm just cautious."

"Sounds pretty cautious to me." He unlocked the door and held it open for me. I peeked inside: beige wallpaper, two lumpy looking twin beds with off-white chenille covers separated by a bedside table, a dresser on which was mounted a WebTV, and an armchair drawn up close to a window looking out onto the roof of the adjacent building. It was like something from the early twentieth century, circa the Great Depression. "Oooh," crooned Brian. "Now this is what I call *classy.*"

"Mom is so going to hear about this." I crossed over to the first bed and tossed my carry-on onto it. I unzipped it and rummaged around for the two sets of I-spex. Brian could be counted on to be distracted by gear. Anything bright and shiny and technological drew him – he was like a techno-crow in that respect. I handed him a set.

He exhaled slowly. "Are these what I think?"

I nodded.

"I-spex. You brought me I-spex? I've heard about them, of course. Too cool." He turned them over and over in his hands, admiring them.

"Let's get something to eat," I said. "Otherwise I'm going to keel over."

He slid the I-spex carefully into one of his vest pockets and buttoned it. "If you ate like I do," he said, "this wouldn't happen to you. I never feel hungry."

"But you eat constantly," I objected. "You never *don't* eat."

"That's because I'm a grazer."

"That's because you're a swarm of locusts. If I ate like you, I'd look like a manatee."

He smiled slyly. "Hate to tell you, cuz, but you sort of do anyway."

I punched him in the ribs. "I do not. Take that back."

I continued to pummel him as he cried, "Uncle! Uncle! You don't look like a manatee. Well, you do actually. A really small, skinny little manatee. Ouch!" He fled to the hall, waving his hands in mock submission. I started after him, then remembered the *lo p'an*. A-Ma had told me to take it with me to Moose Jaw, and here I was in Moose Jaw. "Dump your stuff in your room," I called out. "I'll be with you in a sec." Returning to the bed, I dug around in my carry-on for a moment before locating the cherrywood case containing the geomancer's compass. I tucked it into my knapsack alongside my travel pack of wipes and re-secured the strap on my trusty Zypad armband – the latest thing in wearable technology; never leave home without it. Then I remembered the key A-Ma had given me, the old-fashioned black one; I slipped that into the knapsack as well.

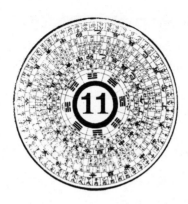

We ate at Nicky's, a little Italian restaurant next door to the hotel with red checkered tablecloths and a not very happy waitress who was, maybe, eighteen. She was probably bummed out about the fact that she had no eyebrows. I know I would be.

"What's your name?" Brian asked. Because that's what he did: made human contact. Whether whatever human he was making contact with wanted to or not.

The waitress did not. She pointed sullenly to her nameplate.

Brian looked at me.

"Svetlana," I read.

"What?" Svetlana asked me, her face slack and her forehead a big blank. "Can't he read?"

"Bingo," I said.

"No tip for Svetlana," Brian whispered cheerfully as she trudged off. "What's with the eyebrows, anyway? Was she attacked by rabid tweezers?"

"Maybe she lost them in a fire," I whispered back.

While we waited for our order to arrive – a Caesar salad with shrimp for me (low carb) and, for Brian, spaghetti and meatballs (high carb; I wasn't Aubrey's impressionable little cousin for nothing) – I told him about my conversation with A-Ma. I mean, I had to tell him sometime.

"Before I tell you what A-Ma told me, you've got to promise you won't interrupt me every two seconds," I told him. "Because that's what you usually do."

"Interrupt you every two seconds?"

"Yes. It's very annoying."

"That's because I have ADHD," Brian defended himself. "As in, not great at paying attention."

"Well, it's really rude."

"I'm sorry."

"So you're not going to interrupt me?"

He nodded.

"Promise?"

"Promise."

I took a deep breath. "OK," I said. "I'm going to start at the beginning."

"A very good place to start. Which is?"

"Which is, I'd always thought the Lius were from

Vancouver, but it turns out we're from Moose Jaw."

"I thought we were from Quongdong Province."

"Well, originally. But more recently. Once we came to Canada."

"Hence the us-being-in-Moose Jaw thing?"

I nodded. "Hence the us-being-in-Moose Jaw thing." So far, so good.

"Which is why The Grandfather's brother is buried here as opposed to in Vancouver? The one whose grave we're supposed to sweep. Old Uncle Fu Manchu."

"Qianfu," I corrected him. "And yes."

"But why now? It's August. Qingming is usually at the start of April."

"Yeah, well, I guess it hasn't been swept in a really long time and A-Ma thought sooner was better than later."

Brian reflected on this. "That's cool. Can we set off firecrackers?"

I steeled myself. "There's more."

"See? I knew you were holding out." He grinned and leaned over the table toward me, his dark eyes button bright, his crazy hair exploding from his head in gelled spikes. He looked like a demented Halloween pumpkin.

I took the plunge. "Qianfu was murdered," I said. "Beaten to death."

"Here? In Moose Jaw?"

I nodded.

Brian considered this. "Cool."

"Not cool," I retorted. "He was our great-great-etcetera uncle."

"OK, you're right. Not cool. But interesting. Definitely interesting. Was it your basic hate crime? You know, a couple of good old boys on a Saturday night looking for some good, clean, angry, redneck fun?"

I sighed. "No, as a matter of fact. He was messing around with a white girl. They worked in the same restaurant."

"I hope she was better looking than Svetlana," Brian whispered, as the waitress emerged from the kitchen with our food, a steaming heap of spaghetti festooned with meatballs and a bowl of romaine drenched in dressing and dotted with small pink shrimps and brown croutons.

"Hey, Svetlana!" he called out. "What do they call you for short? Svet or Lana?"

"My name is Svetlana." Svetlana looked angry, but that might have been the no eyebrows.

"Well, I'm going to call you Svet," Brian decided. "Or Svetty. Like Betty. That's kind of cute, don't you think? Svetty. May we please have a refill on the bread, Svetty?" He held out the empty bread basket. The last time I'd looked, it had been full. That was the danger of eating with Brian. Food disappeared as if by magic – magicians use sleight of hand; Brian relies on sleight of mouth. And he's good.

Svetlana snatched the bread basket from him and stomped back to the kitchen.

Brian turned back to me. "So old Uncle Fu Manchu was murdered because of some girl."

"Old Uncle *Qianfu*."

"Like I said. Old Uncle Fu Manchu."

I started to correct him once again, then thought, why bother? With Brian you have to pick your battles; this was one I wasn't going to win.

"Yum," said Brian, unrolling his napkin with a flourish and tucking it under his chin. He picked up his knife and fork and smiled at his heap of spaghetti the way a shark might smile at an unwary swimmer. (That is, if sharks smile. At the thought of sharks I shuddered. Must not think of sharks, I told myself.) He began to catapult meatballs into his mouth with lightning speed.

"So Qianfu was buried and, seven years later, the family dug him up." I picked up my own fork and scrutinized it for cleanliness. I don't trust restaurant cutlery.

"Uh-hum?" Through his mouthful of chewed beef, I could just make out something that sounded like "Good meatballs."

"Because apparently that's what they did in those days," I continued. "They scraped off whatever . . . I don't know . . . *stuff* was left on the bones and put them in a burial urn and shipped them back to China."

"Wow." Brian was so impressed that he stopped eating for a nanosecond. "That's fairly gross."

I shrugged, trying to be nonchalant. "A-Ma said they didn't like the thought of being buried in Canada. They wanted their bones to lie in the ancestral graveyard – in their village back in China." I wiped the tines of my fork carefully with my napkin, then laid it down and eyed my salad. "This is *so* not the sort of conversation you want to have over lunch." I took a deep breath. *Down, boy,* I instructed my stomach. "So anyway, there Qianfu is, in this Death House ... that was what A-Ma called it." (This in response to Brian's incredulous glance.) "To make a long story short, the Death House catches on fire, the local fire brigade arrives on the scene, and do they freak?"

"Let me guess. They freak."

"They totally freak. A bunch of dug-up bones lying around," I said. "And then, post-freak, they insist on holding the body as, I don't know, evidence or something, and by the time the court rules that The Grandfather can have it back, it's disappeared."

Brian put his fork down and stared at me. "What do you mean, disappeared?"

"Disappeared, as in vanished. As in, somebody must have buried it, only no one knows where. Or at least no one's talking."

"So this grave that we're supposed to be honoring ... we don't know where it is."

"Right."

"And we are supposed to ... what?"

"Find it."

He considered this. "And this was . . . how many years ago did all this happen?"

"One hundred and six."

"So basically he could be pretty much anywhere?"

I nodded. "Yep. Probably somewhere around here, but yes, he could be anywhere."

Brian pushed his plate away, his lips painted with an orange clown's mouth from the spaghetti sauce. "And we're doing this why?"

"It's complicated."

He eyed my salad hungrily.

"Don't even think about it," I warned him, picking up my fork and encircling my salad with my left arm. I began wolfing it down. "How can you eat so much?" I complained between mouthfuls. "Didn't Auntie Ev ever tell you to chew?"

"Nobody chews spaghetti," he countered. "You slurp spaghetti. Now, give me the goods, Randi. What's really going on here?"

"How do you expect me to talk while I'm eating?"

"So, eat. Go on. *Mangia. Mangia.* Chew that cud. I'm going to entertain myself by looking at the tunnel tour brochure." He patted himself down until he found the pocket into which he had crammed the brochure.

"What's the point?" I asked flippantly. "It's not like you can read it." The words were no sooner out of my mouth than I wished I had never said them.

The effect on Brian was like a slap in the face. He flinched. "I'm looking at the pictures," he said in a subdued voice.

"Look," I said quickly, "I'm sorry. I shouldn't have said that."

"Never mind. It's OK. *Fugetaboutit*. It's not like it's not true." He gestured in the direction of my salad. "I mean it, eat." Then he cupped his hands around his mouth and shouted, "Svet! Oh, Svetty! Where's my bread?"

Svetlana rumbled out of the kitchen, full bread basket in hand and looking annoyed.

"Excellent!" said Brian. "I thought you might have died."

She slouched over to the table, thumped down the bread basket, and made a beeline back to the kitchen. Brian helped himself to a piece of bread and used it to mop up his plate as he examined the brochure. "This is weird," he said after a moment.

"What?"

"Why is there a picture of a Chinese dude on this brochure? The gangster I understand, that's Al Capone, but why this guy?"

I leaned forward to peer at the brochure. Sure enough, featured on its front flap was a sinister-looking man in a fedora and below him, against a red backdrop, a kind of line drawing, or maybe it was a woodcut, of a Chinese man wearing a jacket with a mandarin collar and a traditional Chinese hat, the kind that looks like a flowerpot. Under the top photo were the words "Gangster Underground." Below the line drawing were the words "Below Gold Mountain." The words "Gold Mountain" were in fancy Chinese-style letters.

"Give it here," I said.

He handed the brochure over.

"'SEE the past come alive in Canada's most famous system of tunnels,'" I read. "'Go under the streets of modern-day Moose Jaw to discover what life was like during Al Capone's bootlegging heyday in the thrilling, live-action Gangster Underground tour. Then discover the hardships experienced by early Chinese immigrants to Moose Jaw in the moving Below Gold Mountain tour.'" I looked at Brian. "Chinese immigrants . . . like The Grandfather's family? A-Ma never mentioned anything like that."

"This we've got to see," concluded Brian.

For once, I had to agree with him.

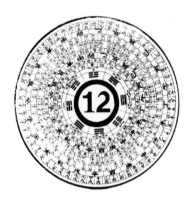

As it turned out, the next Below Gold Mountain tour wasn't for another hour. The next Gangster Underground tour, however, was due to start in fifteen minutes. "C'mon," said Brian. "How else are we going to kill the time?" To which I had no good answer, so we bought tickets to both tours and, following the directions of the woman in the box office, crossed the street to another building and climbed a set of stairs to a second-story lobby where we took our place amid a jumble of tourists.

I stood off to one side, wishing I had a respirator mask. You don't know. Somebody in that group might be coming down with some deadly flu or Ebola fever or something.

Not Brian. He was making the rounds, shaking everybody's germ-encrusted hands, introducing himself first to a retired couple from Cornwall, Ontario, driving an RV across Canada;

then to two American couples power-shopping north of the 49th; and finally to the stressed-out parents of this really annoying brood from Brandon, Manitoba: two scowling tweenies chanting, "We want to shop. We want to shop," and their bratty four-year-old brother who was busy barreling around the lobby like a wood beetle on amphetamines, bumping into people and displays and shrieking, *"Pow. Bam."* He had green snot dripping from his nose. I made a mental note to stay far, far away from that kid.

"And what are you doing here in Moose Jaw?" one of the Americans was asking Brian.

I jerked to sudden life. "Oh, we're just passing through," I said quickly, raising my voice to cover the distance between them and me, and at the same time shooting a warning glance at Brian. I hadn't even begun to sort through the legal implications of our assignment. A-Ma had seemed to think we could just disinter Qianfu's bones ourselves once they had been located, but surely it couldn't be that simple. You don't go around digging up people at will. There had to be some kind of legal process we'd have to go through – warrants obtained, permissions granted. We needed to play our cards close to our chest, for the moment at least, not go blabbing about our mission to strangers.

At that moment a pretty woman in her mid-twenties, wearing a black-and-red flapper dress, a red cloche hat, and a feather boa, burst from a set of double doors at the far end of the lobby. Her makeup was sufficiently theatrical to carry across the distance of the room: emerald-green eye shadow, scarlet lips, even a painted-on mole. She struck a coquettish pose, one hand on cocked hip, the other brandishing a silver cigarette holder, and cried, "Howdy, fellow bootleggers! Welcome to Moose Jaw . . . or Little Chicago, as we like to call it. My name is Miss Marilla and I'm the proprietress of Miss Marilla's Speakeasy, one of Moose Jaw's finest."

I suppressed a groan, shut my eyes, and hugged myself tight. According to the brochure, Below Gold Mountain had been recently updated to include mixed reality. Gangster Underground, however, remained low-tech; animatronics was its only claim to sophistication. This was going to be so lame.

"Cool," Brian whispered in my ear. "It's interactive."

"I hate interactive," I muttered.

"Not me."

"What are you doing standing around?" Miss Marilla cried. "Come on in."

We filed through the double doors into a room meant to reproduce a 1920s bar, complete with a mustachioed bartender wearing a velvet vest and a wine-stained white apron, a piano player pounding out a ragtime tune, and what looked like some drunken dude sitting slouched at one of the several tables.

The tweenies eyed the drunk at the table. "Oooh," they said.

"Oh, don't worry about Pete," Miss Marilla assured them. "He's not going to bother nobody, least not today. Piano player, can you give it a rest while I get these here valuable customers looked after?"

The piano player stopped mid-note; he was animatronic. As for Pete, the snotty-nosed kid came up to him and gave him a solid thwack on the arm. Why do some little boys do things like that? It's like they're barbarians or something.

"Nigel!" His mother yanked him away.

"Ma!"

No reaction from the drunk, however; probably a dummy.

Miss Marilla introduced the bartender, Aloysius. He stopped wiping the wooden surface of his bar and smiled crookedly at the group. "Welcome to Moose Jaw, folks. As you can see, we're a pretty hopping burg, and I'm going to fill you in on our secret. But it's got to be *our* little secret, so mum's the word." I had to admit he was a pretty good actor. He and Miss Marilla both. Maybe this attraction wasn't as cheesy as I had thought.

"In case you haven't heard of it, there's a little something going on in the States called Prohibition," Aloysius was saying. "Yep. Prohibition. That means it's against the law for folks to manufacture, transport, or sell alcohol in the United States. Started in 1920 and it's still going strong five years later. Only, folks got to get their booze somehow, and that's where Moose Jaw comes in. We like our liquor in Moose Jaw and we got plenty of it, both imported and distilled right here in Saskatchewan. We also got us a rail line, the Soo, which runs through Minneapolis to Chicago. Add American gangsters like our boss and you've got what we like to call 'organized crime.'"

"Should I let them in on our little secret?" Miss Marilla was coy.

Aloysius shrugged. "Might as well."

"Our boss is none other than Al Capone, the greatest American gangster who ever lived."

A murmur arose from the group. *"Bam!"* yelled the snotty-nosed kid.

Aloysius nodded. "Yep," he agreed, "you heard right. Al Capone. Old Scarface himself."

Miss Marilla went all conspiratorial on us. "And now I'm going to show you Big Al's room. I wouldn't dare do this if he was in town – Big Al likes his privacy and, believe you me, you don't want to cross Big Al. But since he's in Chicago and all, I figure it's OK to take just a little peek." She crossed the room and opened a door.

The old man from Cornwall turned to his wife. He looked confused. "I thought we were going to have a drink!"

"Hush," his wife said. "It's *pretend*. Like a murder mystery dinner."

We followed Miss Marilla into a simulated flapper-era hotel room, complete with an art deco bed, dresser, and vanity. "This is where Big Al hangs out when it gets too hot for him in Chicago," she explained. "This here's Big Al's spats and his silk jammies –"

All of a sudden a phone rang. It was one of the old-fashioned phones that you see in old movies or TV shows, wall-mounted with a wooden cabinet, a crank handle, and brass ringers. Miss Marilla answered it and after a few back-and-forths, during which she became more and more agitated, she hung up, wrung her hands, and cried, "It's Chief of Police Alfred Humes. It's a *raid!*"

Alfred Humes – my mind snagged on the name. I was sure I had heard it before, but when? In what context? I started to raise my hand like I was in class, but caught myself in time – shades of dorkitude. "Alfred Humes. Who did you say he was again?"

"Chief Humes?" Miss Marilla replied. "Oh, he's the law in these here parts, sweetie, and he's gotten plenty rich by *not* fighting crime, if you get my drift." She winked. "We have a saying here in Moose Jaw: 'In Humes's way? Prepare to pay.' And if you bootleggers don't want to grease his palm, you'd better knock on this door right now and give Gus the secret password." Flinging open a secret panel, she gestured for the group to follow her down a flight of rickety wooden stairs into what looked like an old coal chute. "Hurry," she insisted. *"Hurry."*

That's when I remembered who Alfred Humes was and where I had heard the name before – from A-Ma. He had been the police chief when the Death House burned down in

1915, a decade before the events portrayed in the Gangster Underground tour. Evidently he had stayed on as chief of police and had managed to be as corrupt then as he had been when Qianfu's bones went missing from his jail. "In Humes's way? Prepare to pay." Had somebody paid him for the privilege of making off with Qianfu's bones? Given that Humes was obviously a bad cop, that notion didn't seem too far-fetched.

I stumbled down the stairs after the rest of the tour group, my mind clicking and snapping, barely taking in what was going on around me. Never mind the Gangster Underground. Was the Humes underground a place to start, something we could investigate, something that might lead us to Qianfu's grave?

In the meantime, a secret password ("So's your old man!") was gaining us entry into a facsimile of a gambler's den where a gangster let a delighted Brian fondle an apparently authentic Thompson submachine gun. Then we were traipsing down a damp, dirt-floored tunnel lined with pitted cement to a mocked-up brewery where another actor playing a distiller explained how to age alcohol quickly by adding two or three drops of sulfuric acid to a barrel of fresh hooch. Pretty interesting. Back again to the tunnels, a different one this time, brick-lined, and then we were ushered into an office where an actor playing a bookkeeper panicked at the prospect of a raid by Chief Humes.

Suddenly the lights went out. "Duck!" the bookkeeper yelled. Guns fired. There was the rat-a-tat of a machine gun and the smell of smoke. People shouted and screamed. A siren wailed. "Run!" someone shouted. "Run for your lives!" A distant door was flung open; there was light beyond. "Quick! Quick!" Miss Marilla urged us, shepherding us down another tunnel toward a second set of wooden stairs, dimly lit at its top by a single light bulb hanging from a frayed electrical cord.

Then it was all over, and we found ourselves standing on the corner of River and Main, blinking at the light and shivering a little after the dampness and chill of the tunnels.

"That was good," breathed Brian, beaming. "Even you have to admit that was good."

"Better than good," I replied. "It gave me an idea."

"An idea?"

"A connection, at least. Between Alfred Humes and Qianfu."

"Alfred Humes?" Brian repeated. "You mean, the same Alfred Humes who was supposed to be leading the raid just now?"

I nodded. "He was the chief of police when Qianfu's remains went missing from his jail in 1915, and according to this tour, at least, he had quite the reputation for corruption. So I'm thinking maybe somebody greased his palm a little in exchange for Qianfu's bones. The question is, who?"

Brian slapped me on the back. "Good work, cuz. That super-brain of yours is firing on all cylinders today. And who knows? Maybe the Below Gold Mountain tour will tell us something else we can use. Something tells me it's going to be great."

"Well, it does have mixed reality."

"That's not the reason it's going to be great," he said. "It's going to be great because it's about *us*."

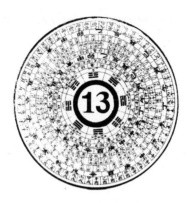

"Please read this over and sign on the dotted line." The cashier handed us each a piece of paper.

"Randi . . ." Brian whispered, with the desperation that greeted any suggestion that he read something.

"Shhh," I whispered back. "It's just a waiver." Since virtual reality began to be widely used in rides and games and simulations, a bunch of people have died or been injured. There were a couple of landmark cases. In one, an old guy suffered a massive heart attack when the computer-generated image, or CGI, of a fire-breathing dragon headed straight for him; in another, a little girl, running away from a CGI green gremlin, fell down a flight of stairs and broke her neck. It didn't take long (or many lawsuits) for enterprises offering VR and even AR, which is much less unsettling, to insist that would-be participants sign a form absolving them in case of accident. "Pretend to read it and then sign," I told him.

"And here is your complimentary motion sickness bag." The cashier handed each of us a standard issue barf bag; it was a rare VR event that didn't make someone throw up, usually me.

"Now HMDs," she added. "Do you know what size you are?" The head-mounted displays were lined up on a shelf behind her; like bowling shoes, they came in a range of sizes. She eyeballed Brian's unusually round head. "You look like a large to me."

Brian turned to me. "HMDs are so clunky. It's like having a watermelon stuck on your head."

"These are the latest thing," said the cashier, defending her gear. "They've got a positioning system *and* head tracking."

"How are we accessing the tour?" I asked.

"Downloaded onto a card."

"We'll use our own I-spex then."

"You have *I-spex*? Wow. Lucky you." Although I-spex were starting to be used in the military and by police, fire, and rescue, they were still not generally available. Unless you had the right connections, of course. "You can download the tour onto your glasses, but wait until the guide tells you to start the program. Launch needs to be simultaneous. Here you go." She handed Brian a card and extended one to me. I shook my head and pointed to Brian.

Brian rolled his eyes. "I'll take it." He took the card from her and held it out to me. I picked it up with the hem of my sleeve. "I'm her toucher," he explained. "Like a taster. You know – the guy who tastes the king's food to see if it's poisoned. She's *so* germaphobic."

"I'm not germaphobic, I'm *careful.*"

Below Gold Mountain had attracted a larger crowd than Gangster Underground. Mixed reality always did. There were the same people who had been on the first tour, plus three beefy football-player types and their girlfriends, and a gaggle of Japanese tourists in nonstop photo mode, despite the fact that they were wearing helmets that made them look like giant, disoriented ants.

The cashier looked up and beyond our heads. "Here comes your guide now."

I turned to see a thirty-something woman, wearing a turquoise mandarin coat over black leggings, and mesh beaded slippers. Her dyed black hair was wound tight into a bun held in place by two silver Chinese hair sticks, and her elaborate eye makeup was meant to suggest almond-shaped eyes in place of the rounder Caucasian eyes she had been born with. The entire costume – coat, hair sticks, and slippers – might have been purchased at the Azure Dragon Tea and Herb Sanatorium. I was surprised they hadn't hired somebody with Chinese ancestry to play the role, but maybe all the Chinese Canadians had left town at the same time The Grandfather had. Given how they had been treated, you could scarcely blame them.

"Welcome, everybody," the guide said. She glanced around the group; for just a second her gaze snagged on me and Brian, then on the group of Japanese tourists. She's taking note of our ethnicity, I thought, our Asian-ness. She's probably received sensitivity training, and of course she can't tell the difference between Japanese and Chinese. As was the case with Oscar, all Asians probably looked alike to her. "My name is Madison," she said, "and I will be your guide on our Below Gold Mountain tour today. Everybody got their cards?"

We all held up our cards.

"*Woo-woo.*" For reasons known only to themselves, the football-player types made a sound like a train whistle, making their girlfriends wheeze with laughter. I viewed them with suspicion and resolved to keep my distance during the tour. At St. Izzy's it was the nerds, not the jocks, who were on top. We had a chess team, not a football team, and that sort of says it all.

"OK, then," instructed Madison, "on the count of three, power up. One . . . two . . ."

I put on my I-spex. "The power button is on your right earpiece," I murmured to Brian.

"Insert your cards."

"Play is on your left," I added.

"And press Play."

We pressed Play.

That familiar jolt of dislocation, followed by the inevitable head spin. My stomach, full of Caesar salad, lurched. I clutched the barf bag tightly.

"Wicked," breathed Brian. "I feel ten feet tall. I love that about mixed reality."

Tipping cautiously forward, I glanced down at my feet. They looked impossibly far away, as though I were peering into a deep chasm at the bottom of which flickered a pair of red-and-white retro Keds belonging to me.

"Everybody steady, now?" Madison asked. "No one's going to lose their lunch on me? Are you sure? No dizziness? OK. We're going to go down into the tunnels now, so everybody follow me, and please go slowly and one at a time. The stairs are steep, people, but there's a handrail on the right. We don't want any stampedes." In recent years, there had been a number of VR-triggered stampedes. Just last year some kids playing virtual paintball in Toronto had panicked in a crowded arcade, run into the streets, and been hit by a streetcar.

The tour filed slowly forward, forming a line, with Brian and me, at my silent insistence, taking up the very end. So far there was no CGI to contend with, I noted. This was a good thing given the fact that we were navigating stairs, which requires a modicum of depth perception.

Like the stairs that led from Miss Marilla's Speakeasy to the gamblers' den below, these were narrow, steep, and rickety, leading to a tunnel with a low ceiling supported by large timbers. The tunnel smelled dank and faintly of sewage, and extended in both directions. A lantern hung from a hook in the wall, casting a wavering pool of yellow light on the packed earth floor. To the right of the lantern was a wooden door. As people jostled for position in the small, crowded space, fog began to roll in, until the entire floor of the tunnel was obscured.

"Is that CGI?" Brian whispered.

I shook my head. "Probably dry ice."

"What you're seeing here is steam," said Madison. "This is how it might have looked back in the late 1800s and early 1900s when the men who tended the boilers that kept Moose Jaw warm during our long, cold winters used these tunnels to get from one boiler to another. And this is how it must have been when Chinese immigrants to Canada, both legal and illegal, were forced to take up residence here in order to survive."

I felt as though somebody had punched me in the stomach. "*Residence?*" I whispered to Brian. "*They lived down here?*"

"*Wow, that sucks,*" he whispered back. He sounded shaken as well. "That's . . . inhumane."

There was a rumbling sound, distant at first, then disturbingly near, and the shriek of a train whistle, followed by the sound of a train chugging to a noisy stop. VR, of course, but incredibly realistic.

"Times were tough in China back then," co
Madison. "The Chinese came to Canada to escape poverty
and famine, to build the Canadian Pacific Railway, and to seek
their fortune in the country they called Gold Mountain.
However, once the railroad was completed, they were left
without work, and the tide of public opinion – never positive
toward the Chinese to begin with – turned against them." She
glanced nervously, first in the direction of the Japanese and
then in our direction, as if trying to gauge the impact this
information was having on us.

It was intense – doubly so because of the VR, which
always heightens feelings, making them less cerebral and
more visceral. Through the spin cycle going on in my head
flew scraps of what A-Ma had said about the reaction of white
Moose Jaw to the Chinese Death House, the uproar and
outrage it had caused, the accusations that had flown: that we
were half human and half devil, that we ate rats and sucked
entrails. Seriously messed up stuff. Somehow it had never
seemed as real as it did right then, standing in that dark,
dank hole in the earth, where rabbits or moles or prairie dogs
might live, or rats, but not human beings.

Madison cleared her throat. "To discourage further
immigration," she said, "the government imposed a head tax
on any Chinese wishing to come into the country. In the
years between 1885 and 1923, the Canadian government made
over $23 million on the immigration tax. To pay for their

fare to North America as well as the head tax, many Chinese were forced to take out ruinous loans from so-called coolie brokers. They had to repay these loans by working for the coolie broker, who would hire them out to slaughterhouses and laundries and burlap factories and take a percentage of their meager wages – sometimes as low as thirty-five cents a day – to cover their room and board."

"Have you ever heard about this stuff?" Brian muttered.

I shook my head. "I knew it was bad, but I didn't know it was this extreme."

"Let's visit a typical laundry of the period," said Madison. "That will show you the conditions under which the Chinese lived and worked back then."

I tugged at Brian's vest. With all those pockets, there were lots of places to grab hold of. "Once I heard A-Ma say that The Grandfather was born in the back of a Chinese laundry. A *hand* laundry."

"What? They laundered hands?"

I poked him in the approximate location of his ribs. "No, Doofus. They washed the clothes *by* hand. Somehow I didn't picture it being underground."

Madison opened the door and held it ajar while everyone filed through into a basement room outfitted like a Chinese washhouse, circa 1900. Through a cloud of counterfeit steam, CGI figures wearing black skullcaps, white blouses, and black pajama-style bottoms labored at washtubs, sewing machines, and ironing boards; the figures had been drawn with vaguely Asian features and had pigtails. The layered effect was achieved through a process called optical see-through – the CGI was projected through a partially reflective mirror onto our real view.

"You'll notice that all of these workers are men," Madison said. "Usually it was the men who came over to Canada and the U.S., hoping to make their fortune and either return to China or bring their families over here. You can imagine how hard that was, given their debt load and miserable wages. In addition, there was a great deal of prejudice against them. One of the reasons they had to live and work down here in the tunnels was so white people wouldn't have to see them."

Brian shook his head. "How bizarre is that?"

"I had no idea," I whispered back. And I truly hadn't. Certainly I had never experienced any prejudice growing up in Vancouver. If anything, being Chinese was seen as a plus, an advantage. Chinese kids were viewed as being smarter than white kids, more talented, better disciplined. Our families tended to be affluent because our great-grandparents and our grandparents and our parents had worked so hard for everything they got. But here in this prairie town only a little over a century before, we had been considered scum of the earth. Worse. Suddenly I did not feel so self-assured, so confident of my place in the world or of my own abilities. If I had been born back then, what chances would I have had?

How would others have seen me? What sort of life would I have been able to carve out for myself, here in this darkness? For the first time, my heart ached for my ancestors. My life was incredibly easy compared to theirs; I owed them everything, especially The Grandfather. Where I had seen a slightly smelly, possibly senile Yoda action doll, way past his expiry date, there had been nothing less than a giant.

Speaking of which . . .

I blinked. An avatar materialized from the steam to the right of my visual field and hovered there for an instant. I recognized it immediately. It was The Grandfather. The Grandfather! What was he doing here? "Brian," I whispered.

"What?"

"Do you see something?"

"What do you mean?"

"Over there, to the right. Do you see an avatar?"

"No. Wait." He leaned forward. "Yeah, I do. That thing with the glowing green globe. Isn't it part of the . . . ?"

"No. At least, I don't think it is."

The avatar floated toward us, passing through Madison and the group of tourists as though they were holograms, and came to a stop a couple of feet away, where it hovered, stooped and featureless. *"Ni hao*, Miranda, Brian," it said. Then, in English, "Hello, children."

"Ni hao," Brian replied in a whisper. "Excuse me, but do we know you? You look familiar somehow."

"Brian! Can't you tell? It's The Grandfather." Because it was an absolutely brilliant evocation of him – hats off to whoever the animator was.

"The Grandfather?" Brian stared for a moment. "You're right. Of course it is, only . . . isn't he dead?"

"Of course he's dead. We were both at his funeral. He's stuck between realms."

"Stuck between *what*?"

"It's a long story."

"What? You've seen him before? And you didn't tell me?"

"It was a virtual encounter," I whispered. "I wasn't sure it was real. I'm not sure *this* is real." I turned to the avatar. "What are you doing here? Can anybody else see you?"

"I've come to show you two something, and no, nobody but you and Brian can see me. And they can't hear me, either, but they can hear you, so keep your voices down."

"How did you manage to infiltrate this program?"

"Shhh." It held a finger in front of where its mouth would be. "Listen and learn."

"These men worked from twelve to sixteen hours a day," Madison was saying. "What's more, their eating and living quarters were next to the laundry. That meant that some of them spent weeks underground, without getting to the surface to see the sunshine."

"Ouch," said Brian. "They were like . . . the lowest of the low, outcasts or something."

"Now, now, Brian," cautioned The Grandfather. "Wash houses were the foundation of the Chinese economy in North America. You could start one up with almost no money or education. Since most white men felt washing clothes was beneath their dignity, they provided people who had just arrived from China with a rare opportunity."

Madison crossed the room. "Let's look at their living conditions." She opened a second door and gestured for the group to follow. We tromped through a room in which CGI coolies cooked and ate their humble meals, and then entered another narrower room lined with extremely uncomfortable-looking bunk beds. Brian, The Grandfather, and I took up the rear, hanging back a little from the main group so that we could talk quietly. After a burlap factory and, a short tunnel away, stairs leading to a Chinese restaurant ("Wong's Restaurant," murmured The Grandfather, "where my poor brother worked."), we returned to the first tunnel and followed it about two city blocks before stopping at another door.

"Ah," said the avatar. Its tone was wistful. "Here we are, at last."

"What do you mean?" Brian asked.

"My old stomping grounds."

"Right now we are directly under River Street," explained Madison. "Chinatown was on the south side of River Street, and Moose Jaw's red-light district was on its north side – gambling dens, drinking joints, and cheap hotels. In other words, this was the *bad* part of town. What we're about to see is an opium den."

"Your old stomping grounds were an *opium den*?" Brian whispered.

Madison opened the door and the group crowded into a low-ceilinged, brick-walled room. The only furnishings were a table bearing a selection of water pipes, and three mattresses on which CGI figures dressed in white blouses and white pajama-style bottoms lay outstretched. "The Chinese brought with them from the old country a fondness for two vices that caused them a great deal of grief in the New World," Madison said. "Gambling and opium. This association with drugs and gaming, along with Chinatown's location in the middle of the red-light district, contributed to the negative stereotype people already had of the typical Chinese male as a gambler, drug addict, and white slave trader." A glance in our direction. "To give the impression that he was fighting crime and to satisfy the white citizenry of Moose Jaw, Chief Alfred Humes made frequent raids on business establishments in Chinatown."

"Hey!" I poked Brian. "Alfred Humes again."

"Hush," cautioned The Grandfather. "Here comes the good part."

"Where we are standing now was an actual opium den, run by a local Chinese entrepreneur who used to import opium from Hong Kong, boil it and can it, and sell it to the United States – before it became illegal."

"You?" I asked the avatar. "Is she talking about you?"

"Of course."

"Wait a minute! You were a drug dealer?" asked Brian.

The avatar bristled. "An entrepreneur. And it was legal back then. Opiates were prescribed for all sorts of illnesses: asthma, appendicitis, coughs, nerves, epilepsy, and diarrhea. *Ai ya*. Babies were given a form of opium to help them sleep. If I remember correctly, both of you could have used a good dose now and again."

"Above us is the oldest Chinese business in Canada, the Azure Dragon Tea and Herb Sanatorium," Madison added.

"Hey, that's us!" whispered Brian.

"The family who owned it moved to Vancouver about the time of the Great War, and went on to found one of the largest Chinese import and export companies in Canada, but they've never sold the property or made any changes to it since that time. And do you know why?" Madison paused. Her expression was serious, her eyes were wide. "Because it's *haunted*."

"Check this out," said the avatar.

Wisps of fog began to collect into a looming shape – part Casper, part Jacob Marley's ghost from *A Christmas Carol* – with bulging eyes, a contorted face, and an elongated mouth frozen in a scream. "WOOOOO," it wailed.

Everyone laughed except the little boy from Brandon, who hid behind his mother's knees, suddenly subdued.

"Preposterous!" The avatar chuckled, rocking back and forth on its heels the way The Grandfather had in life. "Of course, the real ghost is scarier. Much scarier."

"Ghost?" Brian asked. "What ghost?"

"Qianfu's, of course."

I gulped. Suddenly the cheesy ghost effect didn't seem quite so funny. "Qianfu's ghost is . . . upstairs?"

"Of course it's upstairs. That's why we haven't been able to sell the property. You heard the tour guide. We tried."

"You mean, the ghost is real?" I asked.

"Of course it's real. If it wasn't real, we wouldn't have a problem."

"I don't understand," whispered Brian. "Why don't we just ask the ghost where he left old Fu Manchu's bones?"

"Old *Fu Manchu*?" The avatar's tone turned icy.

"Yeah," said Brian. "You know. Your brother."

"His *name* is Qianfu." Then, "You are familiar with the concept of 'yellow peril,' are you not?"

Brian looked abashed. "Yeah. Well, sort of."

"Let me refresh your memory," said the avatar crisply. "There was a time not all that long ago when white people felt very threatened by the influx of Chinese coming into

North America. We were the 'yellow peril' – dirty, immoral, and villainous, a threat to their jobs, their standard of living, and their women."

"I know that."

"And who was the stereotypical villain most often associated with the so-called yellow peril?"

Brian looked a little sheepish. "Fu Manchu?"

"Exactly," replied the avatar. "Fu Manchu. The men who murdered my brother believed that they were ridding the world of a villain – of, in effect, a Fu Manchu. The perpetuation of this myth, of this heinous lie and the racism it led to, was as responsible for his death as the men who shed his blood and the men who protected those men against prosecution and so flagrantly disrespected his remains. My brother was no villain, great-grandson. He was an innocent man, guilty of no greater crime than love. Do not ever refer to him again as 'Fu Manchu.'"

Throughout this exchange, I remained stuck on the idea that there was a ghost upstairs. I tugged at Brian's vest. "So you're buying this – that there's an actual ghost involved?"

"Randi," Brian replied in a hushed voice, "think about it. I just got reamed for racist comments by the avatar of my dead great-great-grandfather, so I'd say yes, for the moment at least, I'm buying that there's a ghost."

"I will need to see you both at the store at, say, five o'clock," the avatar announced.

"At the store?" I repeated.

"I need to determine whether I can connect better with the ghost as a virtual entity than I was able to as flesh and blood," the avatar explained. "Remember that I exist in cyberspace only. Unless a provision is made for virtual reality, I can't go anywhere. That means that, in order to get into the store, I will require your assistance. I also have to determine whether Qianfu is too far gone, whether there remains to him anything human that may be reasoned with or appealed to . . . or whether he is pure monster."

As suddenly as it had appeared, the avatar vanished. It was as though it had been switched off, like a light.

"Are you two coming?" This from Madison, who was standing at the door.

We were alone in the opium den. The rest of the group was heading down the tunnel, back toward the surface; we could hear sounds of conversation and laughter as they moved farther away from us. "Believe me, you don't want to hang around here long," Madison said. She glanced around her, then shivered. "The truth is, this building actually *is* haunted."

"What do you mean?" Brian asked, as we followed her through the door and down the narrow tunnel.

"That's why the family hasn't sold," she explained. "They tried to for years and years, but every time a real estate agent went to show the property, the ghost materialized and scared the prospective buyers away." We started up the stairs. "I'm not a superstitious person but, I tell you, some of the sounds that come out of that place ... people say it's the wind, but it makes the hair on the back of my neck stand up. You might want to turn your I-spex off now. Let your eyes adjust."

"Oh, right." I powered off.

And there it was – that heart-stopping jolt. My mental powers tumbled headlong into a swirling void. I fought rising panic: *Hold on. Hold on. Almost there. Almost grounded.* Then there was a click and there we were, back in the lobby, back in this version of the real world.

"Wow," breathed Brian. "No matter how often I do that, it never ceases to freak me out."

Madison hesitated, then said, "I hope that wasn't too upsetting for you guys. You know. Seeing how the Chinese had to live back then. It was bad, really bad."

We stared at her, dazed.

"Anyway . . ." she added, looking a little embarrassed, "have a great rest of your day in Moose Jaw."

Not bloody likely, I thought.

"Yeah, you too," Brian managed. "Thanks."

"Bye!" And she was gone. Not like The Grandfather – she went through the door.

Brian glanced around. "Where'd he go? The Grandfather, that is."

"I don't know." I thought for a moment, remembering the first time I had encountered him in the virtual tour of the *lo p'an.* "I think the only way we can access him is in a virtual environment. I think he's . . . like, *hosted* maybe . . . on the *feng shui* network."

"Wow." He shook his head. He looked stunned, at a loss for words for once. "That's crazy."

"I know," I said. "It's all really crazy. What time is it?"

Brian consulted his watch. "Four-fifteen."

"We've got forty-five minutes before we're supposed to meet The Grandfather," I calculated. "I've got to think. Sort this out. Do you want to get some Guarana Fizz? I think I'm in serious need of carbonization. I'm in serious need of something."

"Me too," said Brian. His eyes lit up. "*Pie.*"

For some reason – we weren't thinking straight and, besides, Moose Jaw's downtown seemed to exist in some strange parallel universe, a Bizarro World with no Starbucks – we made our way back to Nicky's Restaurant and took the same booth we had vacated a couple of hours earlier. I tried ordering a variety of things ending in "cino" and involving "latte" somewhere in the title; in the end I had to settle for something Svetlana swore was coffee, although I had my doubts. As for Brian, he ordered a piece of saskatoon berry pie *à la mode* and a gigantic glass of milk. "When in Rome," he said, by way of explanation. Then he pointed his fork at me in a menacing way. "Spill the beans, Randi."

"Spill what beans?" I stared at my coffee. It didn't look safe. I opened one of those little creamer thingies they give you at restaurants and poured its contents into the abyss. Then another. Now it looked oily.

"*All* the beans," he insisted. "See it from my perspective. Aunt Daisy collars me when I get home from work yesterday and, out of the blue, informs me that I have to drop everything I'm doing and come to Moose Jaw today to do something very mysterious and oh-so-important with you. 'What?' I ask. 'Your cousin will tell you,' she says."

"I told you!" I defended myself. "We're looking for Qianfu's grave."

"Which is impossible to find. Oh, and then just to mix it up a little, we run into our deceased great-great-grandfather on a virtual reality tour and you say, well yes, this isn't the first time that's happened. What? Did it slip your mind?"

"Of course it didn't. It's just that . . . I told you, Brian. I didn't know whether it counted, whether you could say that an encounter in a VR environment was something that actually took place."

He shut me down fast and hard. "Uh-uh. No. I'm not buying it. You're withholding information. You're telling me what you think I need to know and nothing more. You think I'm stupid, but I'm not."

"I don't think you're stupid."

"Yes you do. All of you. Don't think I don't know it." The look on his face . . . I'd never seen him so serious. Or was that hurt I was reading in his expression? I felt a stab of guilt in my gut. He was right, of course. I had always thought of him as kind of dumb; we all did. "Crazy Brian!" we'd say. What we meant was "Crazy *dumb* Brian."

"You're dyslexic, not stupid," I muttered, looking at the greasy pools of creamer sliding across the surface of my coffee.

"So they say." His tone became brisk. "I'm going to draw a line in the sand, Randi. You're going to tell me why we're looking for Uncle Fu Man . . . *Qianfu's* bones because, in case you hadn't noticed, 'why' is very important. You're going to tell me now. And you're going to keep nothing back. And if you don't tell me everything, I'm finishing this pie – which is excellent, by the way – and then I'm packing it in and going back to Vancouver."

I threw up my hands. "All right. You win. It's because we're cursed. There, I've said it. Are you happy? We're looking for Qianfu's bones because we're *cursed.*"

He stared at me. "Who's cursed?"

I leaned over the table and hissed, "Us. The Lius. The whole family."

He looked baffled.

"What?" I demanded. "You haven't noticed that there's something wrong with all of us?"

"Not you."

"Not yet. Apparently I'm to be eaten by a shark off Bermuda."

"How do you know that?"

"The Grandfather told me."

"When?"

"Yesterday."

"No, I mean when are you going to be eaten by a shark?"

"In three months."

"I wouldn't go to Bermuda if I were you."

I sighed. Shutting my eyes, I rubbed my forehead where a small headache was beginning to percolate. Silently I named this headache "Brian." "Do you see now why I didn't want to tell you? Not because I thought you were stupid. Because this whole curse thing is just . . . nuts, is what it is."

He considered this for a moment. He dug around in his pie like he was looking for something – rocks, jewels, stray bits of beetle. "It doesn't sound that crazy to me. In fact, it would explain a lot of things."

I rolled my eyes.

"It would!" he argued. "And why not? 'There are more things in heaven and earth, Horatio, than are dreamt of in your philosophy.' That's from *Hamlet*."

"I know," I said tartly. "We studied it in English last year."

"And I saw the movie. So let's say we are cursed. For argument's sake. *Why* are we cursed?"

"That's where Qianfu comes in. According to The Grandfather and A-Ma, the *feng shui* where Qianfu is buried, wherever that is, sucks, so he's punishing us. Ergo the curse. What's a ghost to do?"

Brian looked thoughtful. "Bad *feng shui*. That makes sense."

I snorted. "Yeah?"

"Yeah."

"You know about *feng shui*?"

Brian gave me what was probably intended to be a withering look. "I'm a *bonsai* warrior, Randi. *Bonsai* and *feng shui* are complementary disciplines. Of course I know about *feng shui*."

"Well, you know more than me, then," I admitted. "I only know that toilet lid thing."

"So let me get this straight. You're saying that, if we manage to find Fu Man . . . *Qianfu's* bones and rebury them in a place with good *feng shui*, the curse will be lifted."

"That's the idea."

"And then we'll be OK?"

I shrugged. "I guess. I don't know. How should I know?"

"Will I be able to read?" The longing in his voice . . . I'm not going to lie; it made my heart hurt.

"Are you asking me if curse-lifting is retroactive? How should I know? Nobody's spelled it out for me. Maybe it will just be better in the future. Maybe we'll have to make do with our various problems, but there won't be any new ones. Maybe the symptoms won't be so extreme."

"Too bad we couldn't have done it earlier," he said soberly. "You know. Before." His eyes had a stricken, faraway look. I knew that he was remembering the last year of his mom's life, when she could barely lift her head from the pillow, when she kept asking to be allowed to die. It had been hard on us all, but it had been hardest on Brian. His father dead, Oliver holed up in his own little world, and Aubrey so starved that her brain wasn't working right. I tried to imagine how I would feel if my mother kept pleading with me to let her go; even the thought was unbearable.

"Hey!" In an effort to distract him, and in the interests of full disclosure, I retrieved the wooden box containing the geomancer's compass from my knapsack. "I've got something to show you. A-Ma gave me this the night she died."

He looked at me and his eyes lit up. "What is it?" he asked. "Can I see it?"

"Wipe your hands first," I said. "You've got pie juice all over them."

He wiped his hands on his napkin, then took the box and opened it. "Wow. This is amazing. What workmanship!"

"It's a *lo p'an*," I explained, "a geomancer's compass. It belonged to The Grandfather. It came down through the family. I don't have a clue how it works, some gobbledygook about harnessing *chi*, but I was supposed to bring it with me on this trip. Apparently The Grandfather is going to use it when the time comes to deal with Qianfu. *If* we can find a bundle of bones that disappeared over a century ago, which I'm not convinced we can." I took the box from him and, reaching into my knapsack again, retrieved the key that A-Ma had given me. "She gave me this as well." I handed it to him.

"What's it to?"

"The first locked door we encounter. That's what she said."

"Hmmmm."

"What?"

He slipped the key into a pocket. "I wonder . . . are you through with that coffee?"

I pushed my cup away untouched. "This isn't coffee. This is hot water a flea drowned in. Then there was an oil spill. I don't want to think about what would happen to me if I actually drank it."

"Alrighty, then." He rubbed his hands together with relish and yelled, "Svetty! Oh, Svetty!"

"But you haven't finished your pie."

"Precisely why doggy bags were invented."

Svetlana emerged from the kitchen, looking grumpy and hard done by. She lumbered over to the table and stood there scowling and kind of twitchy, like she was spoiling for a fight. I could sympathize. I had often wanted to throttle Brian myself. It was bad enough having your name shortened to "Randi"; being called "Svetty" would be the worst. I decided to give her a ridiculously large tip to make up for it.

"Check, please, *Svetlana*," I said, sliding the *lo p'an* box back into my knapsack. "Oh, and could you point us in the direction of the Azure Dragon Tea and Herb Sanatorium?"

She gave me this look – what it meant was hard to tell, given the no-eyebrow thing, but it didn't strike me as friendly. "Head east on River Street. That way." She pointed. "You can't miss it," she said, with a sideways slide of her eyes at Brian. "It's . . . *Chinese*-looking." The way she said "Chinese" – not nice.

Maybe not such a big tip, after all.

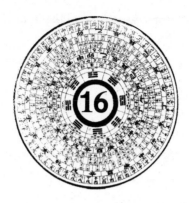

16

We were not half a block from the restaurant when I spotted this homeless man camped out on the sidewalk at the junction of an alley and River Street. A scrawny black dog with a makeshift collar of twine and a leash improvised from a piece of rope lay coiled at the man's feet. I stiffened and, taking Brian by his elbow, drew him closer. "Don't you dare talk to that guy!"

"Why not?" he asked in a perfectly audible voice. Which he did on purpose to embarrass me.

"*Shhhhh!* I mean it, Brian!"

My entreaty fell on deaf ears, of course. No sooner were the words out of my mouth than Brian was making a beeline for the dog. He really likes dogs. I mean, he is over the top about them. I like dogs too – if they're clean and don't drool. I couldn't tell whether this dog was a drooler, but it was definitely not clean.

"Nice dog," Brian was saying to the homeless man. "Can I pet him?"

The man stared at Brian with heavy-lidded, bloodshot eyes, then blinked. He looked startled. "Uh . . . sure," he croaked.

Probably people didn't talk to him much, I thought. Probably they just walked on by, pretending he wasn't there. Either that or they yelled at him to go away. That's what I would have done – not yelled at him, but walked on by, looking everywhere but at him and his dog in the alley. Now, because of Brian, I couldn't very well do that. I had to stand there looking at a homeless guy, which is hard because homeless people tend to look pretty rough, like their lives are rotten, and it makes you sad to look at them – and kind of frightened. This particular guy was First Nations, with copper-colored, deeply lined skin and high cheekbones. He looked to be in his forties or fifties; the hair that poked out from his Winnipeg Warriors toque was almost blue-gray.

Brian hunkered down and held his hand out, palm open, to the dog, which lifted its head and sniffed it warily. "What's his name?"

"*Her* . . . *her* name," said the man. He had a big gap between his two front teeth. "It's Lois."

"Lois. As in 'Lois Lane.' That's a good name for a dog. Hi, Lois. How you doing, Lois?" Brian scratched the dog under her muzzle. She evidently liked this, lifting her muzzle higher to accommodate his fingers. "I'm Brian."

"Name's Elijah," said the homeless man. "Elijah Otter."

"Glad to meet you, Elijah." Brian extended a hand. Elijah hesitated a moment, then extended his own grimy one; it was encased in an old black glove with the fingers cut out. They shook hands. I made a mental note to give Brian one of my antibacterial wipes as soon as we were out of Elijah's sight.

"Do you and Lois like pie?" Brian asked.

The man looked uncertain, as if this might be a trick question. "Well, yeah."

Brian hoisted the paper bag containing his leftover saskatoon berry pie from the restaurant. "Because I couldn't finish this, and I don't think I want to carry it around all day."

"We can take it off your hands," said Elijah.

"Could you? That would be a help."

"Sure," replied Elijah. "No problem."

Brian handed him the bag. "Great. Well, nice to meet you, Elijah. Keep it real."

"Thanks, Brian." Elijah sounded almost happy. He peered expectantly into the paper bag. "Have a good day now."

When we were out of earshot, I poked Brian hard in the arm. "Why do you do that?"

"Do what?"

"You know what I mean. Talk to people like that."

"Like what?"

"Homeless people."

"He had a dog. I had a doggy bag."

"You would have talked to him anyway, even without the dog and the doggy bag. It's embarrassing."

"Not to me."

"It is to me."

"You'll just have to get over it, won't you?" He stopped walking and turned to face me. "Either that or – I know, Randi, maybe all the homeless people could go live in the tunnels, so that decent hardworking Canadians like you and me wouldn't have to see them."

My face flushed. Defiantly I handed him an antibacterial wipe. He had me; we both knew it. He made a show of wadding up the wipe, unused, and dunking it basketball-style into a nearby trash can. "C'mon, Little Miss Bigot."

And suddenly there it was: rearing up from the broken sidewalk, a two-story, wood-frame, pagoda-style building with an upward-turning hipped tile roof, boarded-up lattice windows, and a moon-shaped door leading to a second-story balcony the width of the building. Definitely Chinese-looking, unmistakably so. Svetlana had been right on that count.

I pointed to the sign over the store's heavy wooden double door, studded and outfitted with elaborate, corroded lion-head pulls. A hundred-plus Saskatchewan winters had faded the letters until they were no more than a glimmer of paint on bleached wood. Still, I could just make out the words: *Azure Dragon Tea and Herb Sanatorium.* "This is it," I said. I stepped forward, intending to try the door or peek through one of the boarded-up windows.

That's when I felt it – the cold. You know how, sometimes when you're swimming, you come across a current of water much colder than the surrounding water? Or maybe you dive down really deep and hit this zone of super-frigid water? It was like that: a discernible sudden drop in temperature depending on where you were standing relative to the store. Hastily I retreated back into the warmth of the August afternoon. By comparison, it felt almost sweltering. What's up with this? I wondered. If I'd known it was going to be cold, I'd have brought my new hoodie with the cool CanBoard logo. My second thought was a more sobering one: *Why? Why* is it perfectly warm here on the sidewalk and, not a yard away, freezing cold? It made no sense. I hugged myself and eyed the building with suspicion. There was something creepy about it, something I couldn't put my finger on. I was getting weird vibes from it. I know that sounds crazy, but I was. Usually abandoned buildings are like blown husks, all dried up, empty-feeling, but this one didn't seem empty. It seemed full. Full of what? I felt this little flutter in my gut that I recognized as the beginning of a panic attack. Because, yes, I do have panic attacks. Not very often, but sometimes, and they are really annoying and the last thing I needed at the moment, which meant *I had to calm down*. Breathe, I told myself, breathe. Slowly, evenly.

In the meantime Brian was consulting his watch. "Five o'clock on the dot. Were we supposed to meet The Grandfather outside the store or in?"

"He didn't say. Outside, I guess. Presumably it's locked. Brian, listen . . ."

Brian removed the key A-Ma had given me from his pocket and waggled it at me. "The first locked door we encounter?"

Of course! Why hadn't I thought of that? What other building in Moose Jaw would A-Ma have been likely to have a key for?

"Let's see if it fits," he said.

Again the flutter, stronger this time, more urgent, accompanied by a tightness in my chest. Not good, but I could get a handle on it. "OK but, if it does, don't turn it." I didn't say this so much as squeak it.

"Why not?"

"Just don't, Brian. I have a bad feeling." I hugged myself and rocked back and forth on my heels in an attempt to soothe my nerves. Calm down, it's just a building. *No it isn't.* Yes it is.

"A bad feeling? Hmmm. That's totally rational." Brian walked over to the door and slid the key into its keyhole. "What do you know?" he called over his shoulder. "It fits." Then, "Cripes, why's it so cold?"

"I don't know," I said miserably. "It's like there's some

weird kind of perimeter or something around the building, a sort of cold zone."

"Cold zone?" he scoffed. "Probably somebody left the air conditioner on."

"Don't be an idiot," I snapped. "They didn't have air conditioning back then."

Brian considered this for a minute. "I once saw this show where ghost hunters used infrared thermometers to detect cold spots in places that were supposed to be haunted. The cold spots indicated paranormal activity."

"Brian! Could we not talk about this?"

Then he did it: he started to turn the key. He knew I was freaking out and he just couldn't resist nudging me a little closer to the edge. "*Stop!*" I practically shrieked, before clapping my hand over my mouth and looking quickly to see if anybody had heard me. Luckily the cold zone around the haunted store turned out to be not much of a hub of activity. The homeless guy and his dog were the only sentient beings in sight, and even they were out of earshot.

Brian's face exploded into a grin. "Randi! Don't tell me you're *scared*? Scared of a *ghost*?"

"Don't you dare tease me, Brian Liu!" I protested. "Of course I'm scared. It's irrational, I know, but I can't help it."

His grin widened. "But I thought you didn't believe in ghosts?"

"I don't. But I'm still scared of them."

"You can't be scared of something you don't believe in. That's just silly." He turned back to the door.

"Get away from there!" I grabbed onto his vest and tried to drag him away, but without much success. He's big and I'm not, so it boiled down to me yanking at his vest and pummeling him on the back and trying to grab the key, while he laughed and held the key up over his head where I couldn't reach it. The good news was that this tussle served to distract me and keep me from panicking.

"A-Ma gave us the key for a reason, not so we would never use it," he argued.

"She gave me the key, not you."

"And you gave it to me because I'm a Man of Action, and you're a scared little girly-girl."

"I am not."

"Yes, you are. Girly-girl."

"Please, Brian. Can't we just wait until The Grandfather gets here?"

"But what if The Grandfather's inside?"

"He's not inside. I'm sure of it. That's not the way this thing works." The truth was, I didn't know *how* "this thing" worked, but I must have been figuring it out at some level because what I said next made sense to me. "He needs us to log onto the *feng shui* network and do a search for him."

Brian looked skeptical. "Isn't he just going to appear? The way he did on the tour?"

I shook my head. "No, I don't think so. If we're not in a virtual space, he can't get to us. He needs to be … summoned."

"So summon him."

I considered this for moment. "I'll log on using my Zypad, and we can split the signal and have it go wirelessly to our I-spex. That way we'll have a virtual environment to interact in."

"OK, brainiac," Brian conceded. "Give it a go."

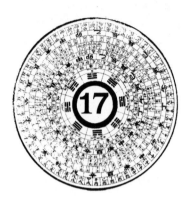

17

First we've got to find him." I crossed to the curb and sat down on it, with my back to the store. Brian hunkered down behind me, looking at the screen over my shoulder. I logged on, entering through the New Age portal and selecting the *feng shui* network. Then I did a control-find for "Charlie Liu." Up came a question: "Do you mean Liu Xiazong?" The Grandfather's Chinese name. Affirmative – I clicked on it.

The avatar wavered into view on the screen, green globe luminous. "Yes!" I removed my I-spex from the knapsack and swiped them with my CanBoard card. "Now yours," I instructed Brian, who fished his set from one of his vest pockets and handed them to me. "I charged them fully before I left Calgary," I said. "They should be good for hours." I swiped his I-spex and handed them back to him, then swiped the Zypad to establish the connection. I took a breath to compose myself and turned to Brian. "Ready to rock?"

"I'm always ready to rock. I'm not the girly-girl."

"Shut up if you know what's good for you."

"I'm not the one who's scared of ghosts."

I stuck my tongue out at him, put my I-spex on, and powered on. So did he.

Because we were not actually entering the virtual environment, but only calling up the virtual presence of a simply delineated avatar, the entry bump was much less jarring than it had been for the Below Gold Mountain tour. Still, there was that sense of dislocation and elongation, as if we had suddenly shot up several inches in height, as if the ground were that much farther down. I glanced down at the screen of my Zypad. The avatar had vanished. For a moment I panicked. Then –

"Shall we?" The voice came from behind us. We twisted around to see the avatar hovering in front of the big double door. In daylight it looked sketchier than it had in the virtual tour of the *lo p'an* or during the Below Gold Mountain tour. Now it was little more than a line drawing, almost cartoonish, in luminescent green ink. It was nevertheless 3-D, thanks to the I-spex's stereoscopic capacity, which gives the illusion of depth to a computer-generated image. Not a bad job.

"My first business venture," the avatar said. It gestured toward the store, its voice heavy with regret. "At the time, it seemed unbelievably grand. We lived on the top floor, above the shop. I can't tell you how hard it was for me to give it up, all that we had achieved, what we had sacrificed so much for. My brother and I were of humble origins, yet we rose from the tunnels to build this business from the ground up. With considerable opposition from our white neighbors, I might add." It sighed and shook its head. "But Qianfu's ghost would not allow us to rest. Not here. Not anywhere. I haven't set foot inside this store since I moved the family to Vancouver, and that was a very long time ago."

"Why is it so cold?" Brian asked.

"Probably a leak from the store. Buildings of that era were not so well insulated as they are now, and there's no place colder than the haunt of a hungry ghost." Brian gave me a look that said, "See, I told you." The avatar continued. "Now, children, before we go in, we must have a little chat."

"A little chat?" Brian repeated.

"A little chat," the avatar confirmed. "I need to prepare you for what you are about to experience. It will likely be . . . frightening."

"How frightening?" I asked. Could I be more frightened than I was now? Yes, I could. Not a reassuring thought.

The Grandfather turned to me. "You, Miranda, will be very frightened. Brian a little less so."

"Why?" I demanded. "Because I'm a girl? That is so sexist."

"No," replied the avatar. "Girls can be just as brave as boys and boys can be just as frightened as girls. You will be more frightened because you are anxious by disposition. Brian is more sanguine; the world does not scare him so much."

"The world doesn't scare me," I insisted.

The other two exchanged glances.

"What?" I demanded.

"Germs and microbes?" the avatar asked.

"How about Ebola fever?" teased Brian. "What about bugs that live in your mattress and are so small that you can't see them without a microscope?"

The Grandfather chuckled. "As I recall, musical chairs scared you." We'd played the game at Aubrey's eighth birthday party and when I had lost my chair, I'd freaked out. Big deal – I was five, and it was totally nerve-racking. You would have screamed your head off too.

"To be fair, Miranda, you are not wrong to be frightened," said The Grandfather. "The truth is that hungry ghosts are far from harmless."

"But they can't actually hurt you, can they?" Brian asked. "I mean, ghosts aren't real. Not in the same way that we're real."

"They are not part of your reality, in the same way that I am not part of your reality," the avatar explained, "but they are no less real than I am, and no more imaginary than you."

"OK," said Brian, "back up. You lost me."

The avatar sighed. "You and I, Brian, exist in the human realm, which is based on passion, desire, and doubt. Qianfu exists in the hungry ghost realm, a kind of hell stoked by the flames of insatiable desire. You summon me into your reality by means of VR; a hungry ghost invades your reality through the extremity of its unsatisfied, all-consuming hunger and thirst, its dire and unslakable need. As for what it can do, it can frighten you to the point of madness or, indeed, to the point of death."

I let out a little involuntary *yelp* – that panic attack was ready to go *boing* at the slightest provocation. Down, girlfriend, I told the rising tide of panic, things are freaky enough without you wigging out all over the ancestral haunted store.

Brian – seeing, no doubt, that I had turned a whiter shade of pale – thumped me on the back. "Buck up, cuz. It's either this or that shark off Bermuda."

"I don't know," I gasped, short of breath. "That shark's starting to look pretty good."

"Follw me," the avatar instructed us. "Stick together and pay attention. When the time comes, do what I say. Do you understand?"

"Can I just . . . stay out here?"

"No," the avatar replied. "You have to keep the connection going and make sure we don't time out."

"But I could do that from here –"

"No." The avatar was firm. "We need to be able to see one another, to maintain eye contact. It's the only way, Miranda. You must be brave." It turned to Brian. "Brian, the door."

Brian nodded, drew himself taller, then walked to the door, flinching slightly as he passed into the cold. He inserted A-Ma's key into the lock. My heart began to pound like a jackhammer and my lungs seemed to shrivel inside me; I had trouble catching my breath. He had to apply a fair amount of force and both hands to turn the key; the lock was corroded. I started trembling; I felt slightly light-headed. As Brian leaned his weight against the door and pushed hard, there was the creak of rusty hinges and the door scraped slowly, screechingly open. Omigod. It sounded just like a tomb in a horror movie.

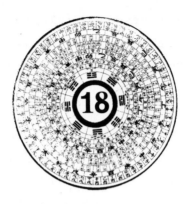

Before us lay a room perhaps fifteen feet wide and twice that long, shrouded in dusty darkness. The latticed windows to either side of the door, the sanatorium's only source of natural light, had been boarded up years ago. The store smelled musty and dank. Again, like a tomb. Great.

"Where's the light switch?" Brian asked, in this perfectly conversational tone.

"Brian!" I whispered. "*Shhh.*" Through the gloom I could just make out gaslamps on the walls, coated in a thick layer of dust. I pointed to one and shook my head. I mouthed the words, "No electricity."

"No point in whispering," the avatar said. It had flickered forward and now hung suspended in midair, halfway into the room. "Ghosts have excellent hearing. They can hear a pin drop across a galaxy."

"It's too dark," I said nervously. "I'm going to activate the Zypad's light source." With trembling fingers I punched up the meter and adjusted the settings on my wearable, bathing the room in a fuzzy yellowish glow that resembled gaslight, all flickers and looming shadow – hardly the bright white light I had been shooting for, but better than nothing. I scanned the room quickly, looking for monsters. Nothing. I relaxed a little and glanced around. Maybe this is as scary as it's going to get, I told myself. You can always hope.

The store's side and back walls were lined floor to ceiling with shelves stacked with merchandise. Directly opposite the door was a wooden counter topped with scales and an old-fashioned, brass-plated cash register. Behind the counter and next to a door leading to a back room teetered a stack of yellow-lacquered coffins, similar to the one in which The Grandfather had been buried. (*Coffins?*) To the right of that door, a narrow, steep staircase climbed to the second floor.

"Would you look at all this *stuff*?" I marveled. Crossing to one wall, I began to randomly read labels: "Peking ducks preserved in jelly, Chinese wolfberry, bezoar . . ." I turned to the avatar. "What's bezoar?"

"The hairball of an ox," replied The Grandfather. "An excellent all-purpose antidote to poison." It was slowly pivoting in place, cane aloft, as it used the green globe to light up the room's dark recesses. *What?* I thought, shivering, my heart rattling around in my chest like a pinball. Was Qianfu's ghost hiding in the cobwebs that hung from the high ceiling? Was it going to drop down on us like a spider?

To calm myself I continued to read my way down the shelf. "Powdered deer horn, potions of pickled wildcat, chicken, and snake, Tiger Balm . . . *Tiger* Balm?"

"Formulated in Rangoon by a Chinese herbalist of my acquaintance," replied The Grandfather. "Good for arthritis and rheumatism, muscular and joint pains, neck and back pain, tired feet, muscular aches caused by stress and sprains. . . . A-ha!"

This caught Brian's attention. He turned. "'A-ha' what?"

The avatar poked at something with the tip of its cane. "Big spider."

Big spider?

"Cool!" cried Brian. "What kind?"

"A long-jawed orb weaver, if I'm not mistaken."

"Radtastic!"

I cringed. "Not radtastic," I protested. "Don't creep me out."

"But spiders are cool!"

"I mean it!" I hit him on the arm. Hard.

"Ouch! OK! Back off, short stuff. That hurt!"

All of a sudden the avatar cried out in a ridiculously loud stage voice, "Qianfu! O Brother! I've come to take you home." We twisted around. The Grandfather was hovering in midair, its arms extended to either side of its head, brandishing its globe-topped cane.

I gave a strangled little scream. "What are you doing? Don't *call* him!"

Brian seized my arm to steady me. "Hey, Randi, that's kind of why we're here."

That was when I first sensed it. Something had changed. Just what it was, I couldn't put my finger on. Maybe it was the atmosphere inside the store, not just the old, bottled-up tomb air, but air turbo-charged in some different and ominous way. It was as though anguish incarnate were seeping into the sanatorium and beginning to manifest itself, to thicken into a presence. A memory of how the air had been just after my father was struck by lightning – bristling and electric and smelling of sulfur – came rushing back. It smelled like a lightning strike had just taken place not three feet from us.

Then my vision dimmed and blurred, the way it does when you're about to pass out – like a gray veil is being dropped over your eyes. I got that sinking feeling of, oh boy, I'm going down. Only I didn't, because all at once there was this crazy loud ringing in my ears, like some humongous bell clang-clanging right beside me – I can't even begin to describe how loud it was. I clapped my hands over my ears and looked up at Brian. He had a finger stuck in either ear and was staring toward the back of the store. I followed the direction of his gaze to the apparent source of the earsplitting roar: there, on a riser about halfway up the stairs, whirled some kind of mini-tornado, about two feet tall.

"What the heck is that?" I shouted at Brian.

"Looks like a dust devil," he shouted back.

The avatar cried out to the whirlwind, "Qianfu? Oh, my brother, has it come to this?"

As if in response, the roar from the funnel cloud lessened and the whirlwind's rate of spin slowed, allowing us flickering glimpses of a faintly human shape with a huge belly and a tiny mouth and throat. It was like flipping really fast through one of those early flip books that paved the way to animation – now funnel cloud, now hideous ghost, now cloud, now ghost. It was gut-wrenching – terrifying and piteous in equal measure.

The avatar cried out, in a voice ragged with emotion, "I have conquered death to save you! Tell me where your bones lie and I will bring them to a place with good *chi.*" (A little over the top, I know, but that's how avatars speak.)

There was a momentary silence. Then the whirlwind began to pick up speed. It spun more and more rapidly, sucking up dust and cobwebs from the room. As it took on matter, it grew taller, wider, darker. Something like smoke poured out of it, filling the room, singeing our lungs and making it difficult to breathe. I clung to Brian, numb with terror. "What's it doing?" I wailed.

The avatar turned to us. "It's as I feared," it said. "What was human in him has been utterly consumed. All that is left is wrath and a desire for revenge. We cannot reason with him. We must master him instead. Give me the *lo p'an.*"

Unable to take my eyes off the ghost, I fumbled for the knapsack slung over my shoulder.

"Oh, for Pete's sake, Randi." Brian reached into my knapsack and retrieved the box. He extracted the *lo p'an* and lobbed it in the avatar's direction. As we watched, the compass transitioned into a virtual object, describing a fiery arc like a comet. The Grandfather caught it neatly and, turning to the ghost, began speaking loudly in Chinese.

"What's he saying?" I begged.

"How should I know?"

Suddenly the funnel cloud, now fully ten feet tall, swung down the stairs and swept across the floor toward us, stopping just short of the avatar, whose outstretched arms appeared to act as some kind of barrier. I shrieked and staggered backward, pulling Brian after me. Once again the whirlwind slowed, until we could make out flickers of the huge-bellied, small-throated ghost, its face elongated in an expression of terrible pain. A hideous noise unraveled from the interior of the funnel, like a scream being ripped into rags. I shrieked again, clapped my hands over my ears, and was just dropping to my knees when Brian caught me by the waist of my jeans, hauled me to my feet, and pushed me toward the door of the shop.

"Brian!" He whirled around. The Grandfather tossed him the *lo p'an*. It tumbled, luminescent, through the air. As Brian reached up with both hands and caught it the way you would catch a baseball, the avatar disappeared in a cascade of pixels.

I pulled open the door. "Come on!" I grabbed Brian by his wrist and together we stumbled outside. Brian slammed the door shut after us, locked it, and leaned back against it, as if to contain the monster, while I stood on the sidewalk, doubled over and gasping for air. I caught sight of the avatar on the screen of my Zypad. Then the connection timed out and the screen went black.

For the next two hours Brian sat on the other bed in my room back at the Prairie Rose, tabbing maniacally through the gazillion channels available to hotel guests on WebTV, lingering only long enough on each one to give me a brief commentary: "The Oxfam Channel. Look. Loads of starving people. Aubrey would love this." Or "How can there be an entire portal completely devoted to corgis?" Ordinarily I would have banished him to his room the moment he powered on the TV, because it's never a good idea to give anyone with ADHD a remote. However, I had just seen a ghost: company of whatever sort – provided it was human and alive – struck me as a positive.

As for what I was doing during that same period, I'd have to say *squat*. Oh, I made a half-hearted show of scanning the reams of geo-coded data I had downloaded to my Zypad before leaving Calgary – land titles and geospatial data, aerial photographs and topographical data, satellite images and the national road dataset . . . but basically I was just doing my deer-in-the-headlights impersonation. *Hello?* If your first paranormal experience doesn't throw a wrench in your day, I don't know what will. For the life of me, I couldn't stop picturing Qianfu's huge belly and his tiny mouth; his ragged scream lingered in my aching head, unfurling like a distant siren.

And it wasn't just that the ghost had scared the bejesus out of me, which it had. It had left something in its wake, its gift to me, its legacy – a dreadful feeling of creeping unease that dragged at me like an undertow. It was as though the ghost had not frightened me so much as flattened me, drained me, sucked out of me all of what was never more than a meager store of hope. I despaired. If what we had just experienced was real, in any sense of that word, I no longer knew what "real" was. How much more exists and is real and matters that we don't see or know? A whole bunch of stuff, if the past few days were any indication. If that was the case, how could we proceed, blinkered as we were – blindfolded? We couldn't. This, what we were attempting to do – finding an unmarked hole dug over a century before in some unknown spot – was futile, a case of too little, too late. A lost cause. We'd never succeed. How could we? And if we couldn't, why continue with this . . . this charade? We might as well pack up, go home, and prepare to meet our various unpleasant ends.

This was what was going through my head when suddenly Brian pulled off his headphones and turned to me. "Enough!" he announced. "I can't sit here a minute longer with my mind in idle. I've got to do something."

I blinked. "What do you mean, 'do something'?"

"'Something,'" he repeated. "Like you. You're doing something."

I shook my head. "Nope. Not really."

He sprang to his feet and began pacing back and forth.

"Whoa, dude, slow down," I pleaded. "You're being way too intense."

He stopped. "I'm restless. Don't you ever get restless? I gotta get out of here . . . get some fresh air!" He turned and headed for the door.

"Where are you going?" I cried.

"Out."

"Out where?" I began to panic. The last thing I wanted was to be alone.

"I don't know," he said. "Shopping. I'm going shopping."

"For what?"

"Things we need," he replied. "A shovel. A bag of some sort. A body bag."

"Where are you going to find a body bag?" I demanded. "At the Bay? At Canadian Tire?"

"I don't know. Someone has to sell them."

"Yeah, but I bet they ask a whole lot of questions first."

"A suit bag, then."

"Won't a suit bag be too short?"

"Dead people shrink. And it's just bones."

I scrambled to my feet and took hold of his arm. "Don't leave me, Brian."

"What? Are you scared?"

"Of course I'm scared. Aren't you?"

"More . . . I don't know . . . perturbed. C'mon, Randi, give me some space. Nothing's going to get you while I'm gone." Taking me by both shoulders, he pushed me back down on the bed. "Just . . . research something, OK? I need to get my head around this thing. I won't be long, I promise." He released my shoulders, snatched the Helio's keys from the dresser, and left, banging the door behind him.

I started up, intending to follow him, then thought better of it. Sitting around doing nothing would drive me crazy. I could see his point. I glanced at the window. It was still daylight after all, and what I knew about ghosts – not much – suggested that they weren't free-range. They had haunts, and clearly the Azure Dragon Tea and Herb Sanatorium was Qianfu's. Which meant I was probably safe at the Prairie Rose. Probably.

I steeled myself and turned back to my Zypad, scanning the long list of downloads. What did The Grandfather think I'd find? Or did he regard technology as somehow magic, and data as a kind of treasure trove? Of course, data *is* a treasure trove if what you're looking for was ever collected in the first place. The burial of Qianfu's bones had clearly occurred off the record. So why did The Grandfather believe there might be a record of it? Or was he just hoping against hope? I shook my head. This was a wild goose chase I wasn't up to. I decided to download all the archives of the *Moose Jaw Reviewer* and the *Times-Herald* from the time of the Death House fire to when Qianfu's body went missing. Maybe I'd find something resembling a clue in those newspaper accounts. It was worth a shot.

No sooner had I initiated the *Reviewer* download than I heard an eerie howl unwinding from the direction of the bathroom. It sounded hollow, like the wail of something not alive, plaintive and menacing at the same time. A second later I was on my feet, ready to let loose a bloodcurdling scream, when I remembered the desk clerk's warning: that the wind sometimes made the plumbing howl. How had he put it? *Like a ghost in a bottle.* I clapped my hand over my mouth and stood there waiting for my heart to stop pounding. Don't be such a sissy, I told myself. It's just the wind. I crossed to the bathroom, peered inside, then shut the door firmly before returning to the bed and my download. "It's just the wind, it's just the wind," I repeated out loud, as I watched the download indicator bar slowly fill up.

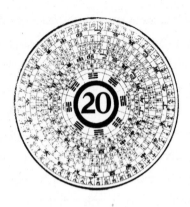

It was eight-thirty when Brian returned, a shovel in one hand and a suit bag in the other. He looked more his old self, relaxed and goofy rather than all conflicted. "Look at this," he said proudly, holding the bag out for my inspection. "Pierre Cardin. Only the best for old Uncle . . . Qianfu. Because we know how finicky he is." He stepped back and scrutinized me. "Hey! You don't look utterly miserable. Don't tell me you've found something?"

I nodded excitedly. In his absence, I had managed to piece together from the archives of Moose Jaw's two daily papers a pretty detailed account of the circumstances around Qianfu's death. To my surprise, it hadn't been all that hard; in its day, it had been *the* hot story, the talk of the town. There had been a lot of ink devoted to it. "I've got a much clearer picture of the events leading up to Qianfu's murder than I had before," I told him. "For starters, The Grandfather was totally right about the Violet McNabb thing being a huge deal."

Brian stood the shovel up against the wall. "Violet who?"

"Violet McNabb, the white woman Qianfu was involved with, the waitress. Just listen to this. It's an article dated August 16, 1908."

Brian hung up the suit bag in the closet and sat down on the other twin bed, facing me.

I cleared my throat. "'The inscrutable, almond-eyed celestial is alleged to have seduced this fair innocent, plying her with the ancient love medicine of opium, with the express purpose first of ruining her, then of selling her into white slavery.' That is before, 'virtuous vigilantes saved this flower of Moose Jaw from a fate worse than death.'"

"Wow," breathed Brian. "That's extreme!"

"And there are photos." I turned the Zypad toward Brian. He leaned forward to peer at the blurred photograph of an unsmiling young woman in her early twenties. She was wearing a prim white shirtwaist with a turnover collar and little buttons down the front, and had big, pale eyes, a long nose, and a wad of sepia-colored hair piled high upon her head.

Brian winced. "If Violet McNabb was the flower of Moose Jaw, I'd hate to see its skunk cabbage."

"Here's a photo of Qianfu." I scrolled down to the image of a young, smooth-faced Chinese man with high cheekbones, squinty eyes, and a slightly bulbous nose. His thick eyebrows, which rose to a peak in the middle, resembled a kid's drawing of a bird in flight. He looked like early portraits of The Grandfather – not surprising, given that they were twins. "What's really Bizarro World is how much of a stink their relationship caused. The Saskatchewan Legislature actually passed a law making it illegal for 'Orientals' to employ white women, period. All because of this one case. All because one white woman working in one restaurant in one hick town was seen holding hands with another employee, who just happened to be Chinese."

Brian shook his head. "I don't know, Randi. Interracial hand-holding, the first step on the road to perdition."

"Evidently."

"So Violet lost her job at Wong's Restaurant and Uncle Qianfu lost his life. That seems fair and balanced."

"Talk about a double standard. A-Ma told me that The Grandfather always suspected the disappearance of Qianfu's bones had more to do with his involvement with Violet McNabb than with public outrage over the Death House; that it might have been an act of further revenge on the part of people who thought being murdered was not punishment enough for a Chinese man who had the nerve to romance a white woman. That's starting to sound right to me."

"So who looks good to you?"

"Well, at first I was thinking about the chief of police. You know, Alfred Humes. But Humes's thing was corruption, right? I think he didn't look very hard for Qianfu's killers, probably because he knew who they were and he went along with the murder. Then, later, I think he probably looked the other way when Qianfu's bones disappeared."

"For a price?"

"For a price."

"So, ruling out Humes for the moment, who else?"

"The McNabb clan," I replied. "Violet's family. They were *so* not happy about the whole Qianfu thing. Violet was absolutely and utterly ruined for life, a terrible shame had been visited upon their family, blah, blah, blah. And that was just Ma and Pa."

"She had sibs?"

I nodded. "Twin brothers, wouldn't you know? Dwight and Dwayne, and no, I'm not kidding. And they weren't exactly the forgive-and-forget type. More the tar-and-feather type. According to the *Times-Herald*, there were a number of times Humes had to lock them up overnight to keep them from doing things like . . . oh . . . torching the whole of Chinatown."

"I thought Humes was on their side."

"Humes was on the side of whoever could pay him the most," I pointed out. "I dug around a little and found some accounts by local historians writing in the 1940s. According to them, the Chinese merchants paid Humes enough in protection money that he had a vested interest in Chinatown being a going concern. Every once in a while he would stage a very public raid on an opium den or a gambling house, but that was mostly show, to assure the white citizens of Moose Jaw that he was their go-to guy for law and order."

"OK, then. Bye-bye Chief Humes. Hello, Dwight and Dwayne. Two identical rednecks cruising for revenge and a good time. Retribution. The restoration of the family's lost honor. All good reasons to murder a Chinese dude and steal his bones."

"Not so fast," I warned him. "I thought I remembered A-Ma saying that Violet had married later, so I searched her name in the newspaper archives and found this." I pulled up an engagement announcement in the society page of the *Reviewer* and read, "'Joseph and Edna McNabb and George and Marianne Rawlins of Moose Jaw are pleased to announce the engagement of their children Violet and Willard.'" I looked up. "The announcement is dated June 1908, a couple of months *before* Qianfu was murdered."

Brian whistled. "Good catch, Randi! A jilted lover. Boy, that Willard had to be some bitter. Thwarted love combined with a healthy dose of wounded male pride, especially since he probably thought the guy she replaced him with was subhuman. That's got to hurt."

"Exactly," I agreed. "But there's more. I also found this." I pulled up a second announcement, dated to June 1914. "'Joseph and Edna McNabb are pleased to announce the *marriage* of their daughter Violet to Mr. Willard Rawlins.'"

"So she actually ended up marrying the guy?"

I nodded. "Six years after the murder, one year before the Death House scandal. OK, but then I got this hunch . . . 1914 was when World War I broke out, and Willard was the right age to go to war, so I went to the government's Veterans Affairs website and did a search for him on the Virtual Memorial database."

"And?"

"Willard died at Vimy Ridge in 1917."

"What about Dwight and Dwayne?"

"They beat him by a year. Battle of the Somme."

I could tell that Brian saw where I was going with this. I wondered fleetingly why I had always thought of him as dumb; he was actually pretty smart. "So I guess the real question is: when did they leave for Europe?"

"According to the Virtual Memorial, the McNabb twins were with Moose Jaw's 27th Light Horse, which was called up in early 1915. Willard was with the 65th and that didn't mobilize until early 1916."

"By 'early,' what do you mean?"

"Oh, I don't know. January. February."

"And when did the Death House fire take place? What month?"

"November. November 1915."

"So Dwight and Dwayne were killing people over in Europe in 1915 when Uncle Qianfu's bones went missing. *And*

Willard wasn't." He looked at me. "That can only mean that Willard is our man."

"It sure looks that way." For the first time, I felt we might, just *might* be getting somewhere. And it was my research skills, my media savvy, that had brought us to this point. I felt pretty pleased with myself, I have to tell you.

That's when Brian dropped his bomb. "I've got my own news," he said brightly. "I've been doing a little sleuthing on my own."

His own sleuthing? "What do you mean?"

"Just what I said," he replied. "A local I was chatting up told me something very interesting. I think it may have some bearing on our case. Just a hunch."

"Well?" I asked, suddenly wary. "What? Who?"

"Oh, you'll recognize him when you see him." Brian crossed to the door and opened it. "Hey, Elijah," he called. "Wanna come in here?"

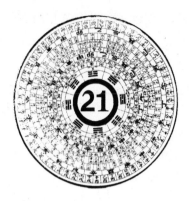

Oh, no!" I moaned. "No, Brian. Not the homeless guy?"

Brian looked daggers at me, shook his head once, and pressed his index finger to his lips before slashing that same finger across his throat. In other words, "Shut up or I'll kill you."

So yes, in answer to my question, it was the homeless guy – who, it was now clear, had been camped in the hall outside the room since Brian's return to the hotel. I apple-dolled my face to indicate my displeasure before falling back onto the bed in mute, grumpy submission. As I lay there, staring angrily at the ceiling, I noticed a suspicious yellow stain that looked a lot like Italy. What was it? Had the toilet in the room above had some sort of flushing malfunction? Was it recent?

In the meantime, Brian had turned back to the door and was saying in this really smooth way – you know, the way you talk to little kids when they won't eat their disgusting squash or try to convince your dog to trade your grandmother's hearing aid for a Milk-Bone – "Come on in, Elijah. No, no problem. Seriously. She's cool." Back his head pivots, in my direction. "Be cool," he mouths to me, scowling fiercely to underscore his point.

"I'm cool," I mouthed back. Might as well be. How long could this – whatever *this* was – take? Get the guy in and out, with a fiver for the favor, and then I could start searching Land Registry for any properties that once belonged to Willard Rawlins.

Elijah's smell preceded him, a rank combination of wood smoke and old sweat, made all the more pungent by the wet-dog smell that Lois contributed to the mix.

Wait a minute – Lois?

I sat up. How had Brian managed to get Lois past the desk clerk? Assuming, of course, that Oscar saw anything wrong with letting homeless people and their mangy pets wander all over his hotel. It wasn't the Ritz, after all.

Elijah appeared in the doorway, looking hesitant, embarrassed, and a little bewildered. He was taller than I would have guessed, almost as tall as Brian. Well, duh; when we had first seen him, he'd been sitting all hunched over but, even standing, he looked stooped, like the upper part of his spine had collapsed in on itself. He must have been a big man once, judging from the broadness of his shoulders and the size of his feet and hands. Now his clothes – an old navy blue windbreaker pulled over a dirty gray sweatshirt, baggy khaki pants with frayed hems held up with a belt improvised out of rope – hung from him as if from a skeleton.

"What are you waiting for? Come on in. Sit down." Brian gestured toward the armchair by the window.

"Lois?" Elijah asked uncertainly. He looked over his shoulder. "I don't go nowhere without her."

"Lois too." Brian was expansive. "The more the merrier. We like dogs. Don't we, Randi?"

I nodded, cringing a little. *Clean* dogs, I thought, not walking three-ring flea circuses. Just the thought of Lois made me feel itchy. But at least it made me forget about the stain in the ceiling.

"It's just that . . . sometimes people don't let her . . . they don't *allow* her," Elijah explained. "That's why I don't go to the shelter. She's not welcome there. They say I can stay but not Lois, she'll have to go to the Humane Society. I know what happens to dogs at the Humane Society, dogs nobody wants because they're old and broke down and not this type or that type but a Heinz 57. How could I do that to her when she's been with me all these years?"

"No worries, Elijah," Brian assured him. "Lois is welcome here."

"Well, OK, then." Elijah eyed the armchair with its faded upholstery and its shiny seat, then shuffled toward it like a big old gaunt bear, trailed by the woebegone Lois. Never, I thought, had I seen a more abject-looking animal. Everything about her drooped, and she had these sad, sad eyes. Tragic, really. Because when you think about it, it's got to be super-depressing being a homeless person's dog.

Elijah glanced out the window at the roof of the adjoining building. "Nice view," he observed. He sat down gingerly, like he didn't trust the chair not to break. (I made a mental note not to ever sit in that chair.) Lois slumped to the floor and flattened herself on the rug at his feet like a furry mud puddle. Elijah rubbed his hands together as if for warmth. "Don't suppose you got one of those minibars, do you?"

"Nope," replied Brian. "Sorry."

"Just asking."

Brian sat on the edge of the bed nearest him. "Elijah," he said, "I want you to tell Randi what you told me out on the street."

"OK. Yeah, sure." Elijah removed his toque. His hair was long, coarse, and the color of iron. He sniffed the toque, then proceeded to knead it as he cast furtive glances around the room, looking nervous and distracted.

We sat there, Brian and I, looking intently at him. After a moment Brian said, "Elijah?"

"Huh?"

"You were going to tell Randi what you told me out on the street. About the golf course."

"Oh yeah, sure," said Elijah. "Ahh . . . remind me." Definitely not the sharpest tool in the shed.

"You were working for a construction crew . . ."

"That's right," said Elijah. "Abbott and Sons. Good job." He turned to me. "I wasn't always like this, you know? Not so . . . down and out."

It was all I could do not to recoil from him. He smelled like old cheese. I gulped and smiled a fake smile, and nodded.

"And there was this golf course development company that wanted to build an eighteen-hole course on the outskirts of town," Brian continued to prompt him. "Weeping Birches Golf Club."

"That's right. Weeping Birches. Big Sky Golf Course Development," said Elijah. "Where Highway 363 heads south going toward Abound and Old Wives Lake."

I turned to Brian. "What's up with this?"

"Patience, Grasshopper. Go on, Elijah."

"So Big Sky bought up a whole bunch of land down there, including this one pig farm . . ."

My heart skipped a beat. I glanced quickly at Brian. He widened his eyes and nodded. "*Pig* farm?" I repeated.

"It was pigs, all right." Elijah's nose wrinkled and the corners of his mouth turned down in disgust. "Been twenty years, I still remember the stink. Never smelled anything worse in my life."

And I bet you've smelled some very bad things, I thought. Yourself, for example. "Did the farm belong to the Rawlins family?"

Elijah nodded. "It did. Was Old Man Rawlins who sold it to Big Sky."

I did the math in my head. Presumably Willard was around The Grandfather's age; if he hadn't died on Vimy Ridge, he would still have been long dead by the time his descendant sold the family farm. "Old Man Rawlins" had probably been his son. Or his grandson, or maybe a nephew or great-nephew. I hadn't yet gone looking for birth announcements in the archives, but Violet and Willard had been married a year before he went off to war; a child might well have been conceived in that year.

"Go on, Elijah," Brian said. "Tell her what happened next."

"Well, Big Sky contracted with Abbott and Sons to take down the outbuildings and start leveling the ground."

"And . . . ?" Brian prompted.

"And that's when we found the grave."

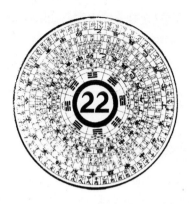

There was a moment of stunned silence. Then, "Omigod," I cried, bouncing on the bed and clapping my hands. "You're kidding. You've got to be kidding. Really? A grave? You found *a grave*?"

My excitement seemed to take Elijah by surprise. Presumably Brian's reaction to this information had been less over the top. Elijah stared at me, blinked (who was this crazy girl?), then swallowed nervously and muttered, "Yeah. In the wallow."

"The wallow?" I repeated. "What's a wallow?"

"Where the pigs . . . you know . . . where they wallow," replied Elijah. "Roll around in the mud. Pigs like that. Keeps them cool."

"And that's where you found the grave? In the wallow?"

"Between the pigsty and the outhouse."

"Man." I turned to Brian. "A pig wallow? Between a pigsty and an outhouse? Talk about bad *feng shui*."

"The worst," Brian agreed. "If you're thinking what I'm thinking and we're right, Qianfu had every reason to be royally pissed."

Elijah looked first at Brian, then at me. "What are you talking about? Fang who?"

"Never mind," Brian assured him. "Go on."

"Well," said Elijah, "I took one look at that grave and the way the bones were and I knew they had to belong to one of my ancestors."

I gave Brian a quizzical look. "*Your* ancestors?" I asked. "What do you mean?"

"Assiniboine."

"Come again?"

"Assiniboine," Elijah repeated. "We are also called Stoney Sioux."

"How could you tell they were Assiniboine?" Brian asked.

"In the old days, it was the custom of the Assiniboine to place the bodies of our dead on tree scaffolds with their feet facing west, toward the Darkening Land. When the tree scaffolds got old and broke and birds had picked all the flesh from the bones of our dead, we would bury them in the ground. There was no sign of a coffin in this grave, no shroud or blanket. And it was shallow, like two feet deep. White men do not bury their dead that way. That's how I knew."

"But that's . . ." I began. I was going to say, "But that's the way Qianfu would have been buried, just bones dropped into a hole with no ceremony and nothing to say who or what he might have been," but I thought better of it. Better to play our cards close to our chest. "Go on," I said.

"The foreman sent us home for the day," said Elijah. "That's what you have to do when human remains are found. Check with the police, see if anybody's missing. If the grave looks like it might be old, you have to check with the government, maybe the Heritage Department." Elijah shook his head. "But I didn't trust Abbott and Sons or Big Sky, neither. I thought they might try to cover it up . . . you know . . . destroy the evidence, pretend it never happened, maybe slip us some cash so we wouldn't say nothing. The last thing they wanted was a work stoppage. That job was gonna make everybody a lot of money. And I understood that. I did. But I'm Assiniboine. I couldn't just stand by, knowing what I knew, and let my ancestors be disrespected. A burial ground is a sacred place; it should be respected and left untouched. How would you feel if somebody messed with your dead? Ever think of that?"

Brian and I exchanged looks. "Actually, yes," I said.

"So you understand," said Elijah.

Oh yes. "What happened next?" I asked.

"I got in my pickup and headed out for the reserve so I could tell the elders."

"The who?"

"The elders. The tribal elders. At the reserve down at Old Wives Lake."

"And what did the elders do?" Brian asked.

"They filed a claim on that part of the land, saying it was the site of an ancient Indian burial," Elijah replied. "You tell it from here," he muttered to Brian, his voice thickening. "You know. What I told you."

Brian nodded and, reaching out, squeezed his arm. Ugh. He turned to me. "Everything came to a halt," Brian told me. "Development was frozen. A couple of years later, Big Sky negotiated a deal with the tribe; money changed hands and Big Sky ended up building their golf course after all, but around the grave. They planted a bunch of berry bushes around what had been the wallow. What kind of bushes, Elijah?"

"Saskatoon bushes," muttered Elijah.

"They also put up a marker with a plaque, saying it was an ancient Assiniboine burial site. But Elijah here, he's had a pretty hard time because of that grave." He glanced sympathetically at Elijah, who I was pretty sure was fighting back tears.

"Got sacked," Elijah said roughly. He shook his head. "Haven't worked since. Word gets out, you know. Nobody hires a whistle-blower. I lost everything. I was making it good in the white man's world. Then I wasn't. Then I was a failure." He shrugged. "Too ashamed to go back home to the rez, so I stayed here, where I got nothing, where I *am* nothing. And it's gone downhill from there." Bending down, he stroked the dog's bumpy head intently. She lifted her muzzle and gazed up at him in mute canine devotion. For an instant it was like one of those Hallmark moments, all in soft focus and entitled "Man's Best Friend." Tears started to my eyes. Don't be ridiculous, I chided myself. Keep it real. You're looking at a wino and a stray, a bum and a mutt, that's all.

Brian glanced over at me. "Got what you need?"

I nodded.

"OK then." He turned to Elijah. "Hey, Elijah?"

Elijah looked up, blinking. His heavy-lidded, bloodshot eyes shone wetly. Brian reached into one of the pockets of his vest, retrieved his wallet, and handed Elijah what looked like a pretty big wad of cash.

Elijah gazed at it raptly, like it was the keys to the kingdom or something. "Hey, man, thanks."

"Don't mention it," said Brian. "Get something to eat. Get Lois a nice bone."

"I will, man. I will." Elijah stood and tugged on the improvised leash. Lois wobbled to her feet.

"Better yet, why don't you go back to the rez?" Brian suggested. "Go home. Get straight. You've got no reason to be ashamed. You kept the grave of one of your ancestors from being desecrated, even though it cost you big time. In my books, that makes you a hero."

Elijah shook his head. "I don't know, man. I don't know if I can. Get straight, I mean. It's been a long time. Maybe in another lifetime."

"Just think about it. OK?"

"Sure, man," Elijah mumbled. "Can't thank you enough. C'mon, Lois." Together they shuffled from the room and made their way down the hall. A moment later, the elevator bell dinged.

"How much did you give him, anyway?"

"Three hundred," replied Brian. He pushed his fingers through his hair, spiking it.

"Brian! He'll just use it to buy alcohol or drugs."

"Let him," said Brian. "The way I look at it, Uncle Qianfu's grave – if it *is* Uncle Qianfu's grave – may have cost the poor guy the best part of what was shaping up to be a decent life. And for what? For what could turn out to be someone else's ancestor's bones."

"Still." I hated the thought of Elijah Otter blowing that three hundred dollars. I much preferred the thought of me hoarding it.

"Look at it this way, Scrooge McDuck. If Elijah Otter hadn't blown the whistle on that grave, whoever's buried there would have ended up in some landfill somewhere. And if that somebody was Qianfu, then good luck finding him EVER. The way I figure it, we owe Elijah big time. In any case, I wish we could do more for him." He studied the floor for a moment, his brow furrowed. I had never seen him like this – so serious.

"You gave him money," I pointed out. "What more can you do? You can't help people who won't help themselves."

He shook his head. "It's not that simple, Randi. Sometimes people need someone to believe in them." He sat down on the chair Elijah had just vacated and, placing his elbows on his knees, cupped his forehead in his hands.

"Get up! Get up!" I cried.

"What?"

"That chair! You don't want to sit there. It might be infested."

"Infested with what?"

"I don't know. Bedbugs? Fleas? Head lice? Cooties?"

"Because Elijah sat here? Wow." The look on Brian's face was ... well, it didn't do much for my self-esteem. "You certainly could never be described as a bleeding heart. Anybody ever tell you that?"

I felt both irritated and really bad – irritated because I was itching to get to work, but Brian was going all sensitivo hobophile on me; bad because, well, it's pretty clear I'm a jerk. "Look, Brian," I said, "I'm sorry I'm not a more sympathetic person. I'll try to be better. But we have a job to do. Let's do it, OK?"

"Yeah, sure." He roused himself as a dog will, shaking itself awake. "Let's do it. What's first?"

"Well, for starters, there's no way we can know for certain that it's Qianfu buried there and not some random person. Right?"

"We could run a DNA test on the bones once we've dug them up," replied Brian. "Apart from that, no. We just have to chance it. The circumstantial evidence is pretty compelling though. I'd say it's worth a shot."

"I'd say it's not only our best shot, it's our *only* shot," I agreed. "So how about starting with the Land Registry? Since all of this happened during the homesteading period – between 1872 and 1930 – I'm going to try the Saskatchewan Homestead Index first." I entered the name "Rawlins" and up popped a file number: 1212130. "Yes!" I clicked on the file number, then whistled through my teeth. "Double score. Look at this." Without taking my eyes off the Zypad's screen, I patted the bed beside me. Brian sat down and peered at the screen. I refrained from pointing out that whatever critters had made the journey with him from chair to bed were now on *this* bed. Instead, I made a mental note to sleep in the *other* bed. "See?" I pointed to the screen. "Where Highway 363 makes that ninety-degree turn, that's the farm, all ninety-four acres of it. See the change in ownership that happened back in 2001 – a single title transfer from Peter W. Rawlins to Big Sky Golf Course Development?"

"So far, so good."

"All Native land claims and related locks were geo-coded

into the Geological Survey years ago, and from there they were incorporated into the Geographic Web layer of Google Earth. Even if the claims are resolved, they stay in the database. All we need are the coordinates of the Rawlins property and we should be able to pinpoint the location of the grave to within a few yards."

"And how do we do that?"

I smiled. "Observe the master." Switching apps to Google Earth, I typed in the address, zoomed in to street level, and enabled the Labels layer. I clicked on the Native Land Claims icon – a single red feather. Up it came, right where it should be. I pulled open the drawer in the bedside table, extracted a piece of aged yellow hotel stationery, copied down the numbers, and showed them to Brian. "*Ta-da.*"

"*Ta-da* what?"

"*Ta-da!* Here we have the grave's latitude, ladies and gentlemen: fifty degrees, twenty-two minutes, and thirty-six seconds north; and the longitude: one hundred and five degrees, forty-one minutes, and four seconds west."

"That's cool in theory, but how do we go about finding this location in the real world?"

"Through the magic of GPS," I replied. "We dial the coordinates into our I-spex and let them lead us straight to where we have to dig."

Brian snapped his fingers. "I just remembered something."

"What?"

"Base maps."

"Excuse me?"

"Base maps," he repeated. "Every golf course has one. It's a data file containing information specific to that particular course – data like tree canopies, bodies of water, watercourses, roads, property lines, utilities, toilets, the distance between tees . . . that sort of thing."

"What about it?"

"It's geo-coded data, genius. We download it from the International Golf Course Database, then layer it over our coordinates using Google Earth and, *voilà*, we know exactly where the grave is in relation to Weeping Birches' other features."

"What do you mean?" I asked. "We already know where the grave is."

"We know its latitude and longitude, but we don't know what hole it's near, or sand trap, or water feature. For that we need the I-spex, and no golf course lets you use any kind of HMD unit because of all the injuries from registration errors. You remember. People kept hitting other people in the head with balls."

I stared at him. "How do you know this stuff?"

"I don't only torture trees. I'm a landscaper too."

"Well, hey, I guess it's worth a shot." I typed the address into Google's search field and soon located the Weeping Birches base map, imported it into Google Earth, and layered it over the grave's coordinates. I zoomed in.

"There it is," said Brian. "Do you see? Right there. Just beyond the fourth hole. So how are we going to handle the logistics?"

I looked at him. "What do you mean by 'logistics'?"

"Like the fact that the grave is in a working golf course full of people playing golf – hello! As far as the law is concerned, this matter has been well and truly settled."

"I don't know. We notify the authorities, I guess."

He laughed. "You think two sixteen-year-olds from out of town can just waltz in to whoever and explain that Elijah and his tribal elders might have been mistaken and the bones might belong to one of *our* relations who, incidentally, has been haunting our family for over a century so, if you don't mind, we'll just dig him up and try and scrape a little DNA off of him to see whether our hunch is right? Is that what you're thinking?"

I scowled at him. In fact, that had been my plan – to the extent that I actually had a plan. When he put it that way, however, I realized how lame and undoable it was. "Did anyone ever tell you that you are a total buzzkill?"

"Just being practical," said Brian. "Sorry, cuz. I know that's your gig, but we gotta suss out the situation, know what I mean? Get the lay of the land. Reconnoiter." He smiled broadly, which made him look like the Cheshire cat. "I hate to be the one to break it to you, but we're going to have to play golf."

I stared at him. "Golf? No, no. We don't do golf, Brian. You know that." Since Dad had been struck by lightning on the golf course all those years ago, the Lius had sworn off golf – to my great relief, I might add. I had never seen the point of golf and, besides, I sucked at it. Nobody had said anything about a ban on golf. It was a tacit agreement, but no less understood for not being official. No Liu had picked up a golf club in years. At least, that was what I had always thought.

"Confession time," Brian admitted. "Every so often, I've been known to hit the greens for a few rounds."

"Brian!"

"Haven't been struck by lightning once."

"It only takes once. You know that. Dad's like a vegetable on two legs. Do you want that to happen to you?"

He laughed. "Hey, I've already got my curse – dyslexia – remember? Why would I get struck by lightning?"

"That's fine for you. But I haven't been eaten by the shark yet."

"Eaten by a shark, struck by lightning. Either way you end up dead . . . or as good as dead. Besides, how else are we going to get on the course?"

"We show up and start walking."

"But you can't do that," Brian protested. "People don't walk on golf courses."

"Of course they do. That's what the trails are for."

"Those aren't trails, they're *cart* paths. And what happens when we get to the grave site at the fourth hole? We have to have some excuse for going into that berry patch. You know how golfers feel about civilians off-roading? They *yell* at them. That's before they bean them. Do you know how many people are seriously injured by flying golf balls every year? Close to half a million. And that's just North America."

I threw my hands up in the air. "OK, you win. I'll do it. I'll play golf."

He beamed. "No, *I'll* play golf," he corrected me. "As I recall, you totally suck at golf. I, on the other hand, have a pretty decent swing." He was right, of course; he had always had a good swing. In fact, he was a sort of natural athlete all round, quickly mastering physical skills that I had found daunting or impossible – skiing and snowboarding, diving and surfing, skateboarding. . . . It was very annoying.

"Whatever."

"So first thing tomorrow morning, I'll call for a tee time and we'll head over to the course. Deal?"

"Deal," I muttered.

Brian stood and stretched. Dropping his chin to his chest, he surveyed his stomach. "Hmmm. You know, it's starting to feel a whole lot like dinnertime."

I checked my watch. "Nine-twenty."

"Care to join me for a bite to eat?"

"Nah." I changed beds and lay down, closing my eyes. The headache that always seemed to be lurking there, waiting behind my eyes, flared. "Could you just pick something up for me? I'm nursing a headache."

"Doggy bag for one. Got it."

"And could you shut off the lights when you leave?" I rolled into a fetal position, knees pulled in close to my body and arms folded, hugging myself. The room seemed suddenly drafty. I felt cold in my bones, and shivered. "It's frigging freezing."

"The Prairies," said Brian. "Not exactly the tropics. Want a blanket?"

"Please. All of a sudden I'm really chilly. Don't know why."

He retrieved a shaggy beige blanket from the top shelf of the closet and draped it over me. I huddled beneath it, trying hard not to think of the bedbugs it might be home to. He turned off the lights. I heard the door latch click into place, and then the lock.

Later, I woke with a start, my head pulsating with a firmly established headache, to hear once more the plaintive wail of the bathroom pipes. It was hard to believe that such a mournful, tormented sound came from anything other than a human being . . . or something that had once been a human being. I grabbed a pillow from the other bed, planted it firmly over my ear to blot out the wail, and fell asleep once more, my dreams tangled up like garter snakes in one of those creepy breeding balls.

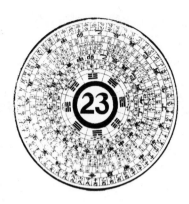

"No, you look good," Brian assured me in a whisper. "Really. It's amazing to see you out of uniform for once. Who'd have known you were a girl?"

"Stop!" I insisted. "I look *ridiculous*." I scowled at my reflection in the long mirror. Wouldn't you know it? Weeping Birches Golf Club had a strict dress code, so ixnay on everything Brian and I had packed (make that everything I owned) and away we went to the club's pro shop to purchase "proper golf attire." My wardrobe runs to black, navy, gray, and olive drab, so the prospect of so much pastel made me go catatonic. In the end, it was Brian who picked out our clothes – or, as he insisted on calling them, our outfits. To make matters worse, they were identical: plaid Bermuda shorts into which a canary-yellow Lacoste shirt was tightly tucked, knee-high white socks, white-and-gold soft-spike golf shoes, light-gray gloves with leather palms and mesh uppers, and a straw visor.

"I think we look sporty," Brian said, smiling at his reflection.

"I think we look like Tweedledum and Tweedledee!"

"Nah," he said cheerfully. "More like killer bees." He consulted his watch. "Tee time in ten. Let's grab some clubs and a couple of PTDs." By PTDs he meant Segways – those two-wheeled, self-balancing Personal Transportation Devices that were so retro they were cool again.

I shook my head in disbelief. He was looking forward to this! What was *wrong* with him? Here I was, suffused with dread and so rattled that my teeth ached . . . and Brian was looking forward to a jolly round of golf! I looked at my hands in their silly gloves. At least I didn't have to worry whose icky-sticky hands had last sweated on the Segway's handles.

Ten minutes later, I caught up with Brian at the tee for the first of nine holes. While I had been struggling to fasten the strap of my helmet, he had taken off at warp speed . . . or what passed for warp speed on a Segway, a raging twelve miles an hour. "What were you trying to do?" I demanded. "Beat some NASCAR record? Vehicular homicide?"

"What can I say? I have a need for speed." He surveyed the hole with approval. Guarded by ponds to either side, it was wide and open, with a gentle slope downhill and to the left. "Now, this is what I call a pretty sight."

"I agree with Mark Twain," I muttered. "'Golf is a good

walk spoiled.'" As far as I'm concerned, there are two kinds of people in the world: people who like games and people who hate games. I am a person who hates games. What's the point if it isn't real? Mind you, events of the last several days had pretty much wrecked my concept of what was real and what wasn't.

"Don't poop on my parade. Ladies first."

"Do you know what you are? You're obnoxiously cheerful."

"Thank you, ma'am."

"That's not a compliment." Still grumbling, I placed a ball on the tee. I remembered that there was a right way to set up a swing, a skill I had yet to perfect when my father's accident put the kibosh on golf lessons. What I didn't remember was how that right way was. This was painfully obvious when I fanned the ball three times before actually making contact. Even that was pathetic. The ball hopped into the air, dropped like a stone, and dribbled into the rough.

"Randi, Randi," Brian cooed. "You've got to let me work on your alignment –"

"No! I don't care about my stupid alignment. Just hit your ball and let's get out of here!" By this time a foursome of golfers was crowding us – like when you're stuck between monster trucks on a highway and they kind of waffle across the white line into your lane and you think, omigod I'm gonna die. They were big, bulky, businessman types, pink with sun, and boisterous.

"Why are you so jumpy?" Brian asked.

"Why aren't you?"

"Because there's nothing to be jumpy about."

"Yes there is. Oh, man! Just hit the ball and let's get out of here."

Brian placed a ball on the tee, took his stance, made a couple of practice swings, then swung for real, hitting the ball right in its sweet spot. It sailed through the air and onto the fairway. He turned to me, gloating. "Now, your –"

"Nope," I snapped. "No way. I don't want this to take any longer than it has to." I plucked my ball from the rough, got on my Segway, and chugged resolutely in the direction of the fairway.

"Eat my dust," cried Brian, zipping ahead of me.

We quickly negotiated the next two holes, the foursome hot on our heels due to my continued fanning. I'm not what you would call a connoisseur of golf holes. Brian, it turned out, was. He insisted on describing their various features – their swales and berms and sand traps and bunkers – despite my frequent, irritated assertions that I didn't *care*. Brian was an unstoppable juggernaut when it came to this sort of thing.

Then we arrived at the fourth hole.

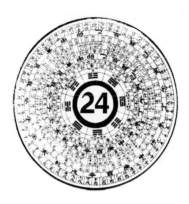

And that right there, if I'm not mistaken, is what we've been looking for." Brian pointed to the left of the hole, between its fairway and the next one. I consulted the course map. The strange eruption of earth he was pointing at corresponded to the spot marked "Ancient Native Grave Site." It didn't look like a berm so much as a big mound of mud that had been leveled off and planted with tall bushes. Could this actually be the point of origin of our family's misery over the generations – this pile of dirt, this messy scramble of bushes? If it was, I don't know what I had expected. Something more impressive, I guess – something more sinister.

"Saskatoon-berry bushes," Brian was saying. "You have to prune them ruthlessly. They make for a good hedge. We're going to need shears."

"Shears?"

"Hedge clippers." He shook his head. "Oh, man. Talk about adding insult to injury! Whoever this poor dude was, he wasn't only buried in a place with lousy *feng shui*, the *feng shui* still sucks even after they built a golf course around him."

"What do you mean?"

"This hole. It's a disaster. The balance is all off."

"I don't get you."

"I'm talking about aesthetics. Whoever designed this hole bungled it. The shaping is horrific. It's what you call a dog squeeze, golf course archi-torture."

"Brian!"

"I mean it. The guy was way too bunker-happy, and look at that monster hogback, right there." He pointed to a large mound in the green. "It's completely out of scale. And the hazards . . . way too tight."

"If you say so. As far as I'm concerned, a golf hole is a golf hole is a golf hole."

Brian shook his head. "No," he said, "you're missing my point. Whoever this guy was, he was buried in a hog wallow, right?"

"Right."

"Bad *feng shui*."

"Apparently!"

"If it really is Qianfu who is buried here and if the landscaping and architecture of the site had been in harmony with the rules of *feng shui*, we might never have had this problem in the first place. But they *aren't* in harmony. Just the opposite."

"I don't follow."

"The grave is on top of a steep incline. That in itself is bad. *Chi* can't accumulate or settle; it can only run downhill."

"*Chi* being positive energy."

"Right. Then there's the cart path. Up until this hole, it's kind of meandered around. Right?"

"Right."

"But for the last hundred yards or so, it's ramrod straight. That's what you call a *shar* in *feng shui*, a 'poison arrow.' Evil travels along straight lines, and this one's pointed directly at the grave."

So it was. "And?"

"And last but far from least, the proximity of that 'comfort station' over there." He waggled a finger in the direction of a vividly turquoise, slightly tipsy-looking porta-potty to the left of the hole. He shook his head. "Toilets and *chi* . . . not a good combination. I'd be pissed too. You know what I think?"

"What?"

"I think we should climb up there and take a closer look at the grave."

My heart set off at a gallop. Blood rushed to my head. Then I heard gabbing – it was the foursome of businessmen on their Segways closing in on us.

Brian snapped his fingers. "Shoot. Too late. I guess it will have to wait until tonight."

I can't wait, I thought. *Not.*

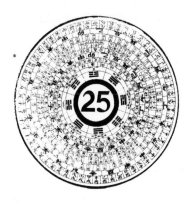

Brian pulled the Helio off Highway 363 into a ragged copse of Manitoba maple on the far side of the road from the golf course; we were maybe five hundred yards from its entrance. Before stowing our luggage in the car's trunk and checking out of Scarface's old haunt, we had changed out of our "proper golf attire" and back into our civvies at the Prairie Rose—jeans and my CanBoard hoodie for me, cargo pants and photographer's vest for Brian. I figured we'd get one chance and one chance only to dig up Qianfu's bones. Either we would die trying or, miracle of miracles, we'd succeed, in which case the plan was to get out of town, and I mean pronto. There was a drop box for the Salvation Army next to the hotel. On the way to the car I crammed the rolled-up Bermuda shorts and yellow golf shirt into the box, followed by the socks and gloves and visor and, to top it all off, the white-and-gold shoes.

"Hey!" Brian objected. "What are you doing? That's good stuff."

"Which someone else will appreciate more than I ever will," I told him. "Because if there's one thing this day has taught me, it's that, whatever else happens, *that* was my last golf game."

The sun had set moments before – according to my Zypad, at precisely 8:21 p.m. Soon it would be dark enough for us to venture onto the course without being seen, but for now the western horizon glowed vibrant pink. "We're lucky there's no moon tonight," Brian said. I didn't feel lucky. It's hard to feel lucky when you're freaked out. And sore? Man! Over my protests, he had insisted on playing out the full nine holes; he had begged and pleaded for the whole eighteen, but I had gotten on my Segway and headed back to the clubhouse, so he didn't have much choice except to follow.

"It's a good thing I don't have to dig," I grumbled. "My shoulders are killing me."

"Are you kidding? I'm just getting warmed up," Brian assured me, beaming. How could he be so cheerful? What was wrong with him? "Equipment check. Shovel?"

"Check. In the trunk."

"Clippers?"

"Also in the trunk." After our golf game, we'd made a detour to Canadian Tire to buy the clippers. Oh, and junk food for Brian; the many pockets of his cargo pants and his vest were stuffed with bags of chips and candies and crackers and peanuts. He was like a walking, breathing snack machine.

"I-spex?"

"Check."

"Suit bag?"

"Check."

"*Lo p'an?*"

I patted my knapsack. Through the thin leather, I could feel the outline of the cherrywood box containing the compass. "And I'm wearing the Zypad in," I told him.

"What for?"

"To make sure somebody's really down there," I replied. "Since the grave site's in the database, we should be able to use WorldBoard's infrastructural anatomy function to see the grave's contents. Once we're in position."

"Good thinking. No point digging if nobody's down there."

"I just wish we knew for sure if it was Qianfu," I said.

"It's our best – heck, it's our *only* option," Brian replied.

"I know," I said, "but it doesn't make me feel any better about trespassing on private property and disturbing a grave site and whatever other crimes we're about to commit."

We sat for a moment, our eyes fixed on the pink horizon. Brian extracted a bag from one of his pockets. "Jujube?" he offered.

I shook my head. I don't like jujubes and, even if I did, I don't think I could have swallowed one at that moment. It felt as though invisible hands wrapped around my neck were slowing squeezing my windpipe closed. "What kind of security do golf courses have, anyway?"

"Video surveillance," replied Brian, chewing. "I spotted some cameras today, but whoever's doing the monitoring is probably just focussing on the Segway stand and the bag drop – that's where thefts happen. Mind you," and he gave me a sideways glance, "I *was* thinking of stealing a Segway . . ."

"Brian!"

"But we've got all this gear to lug!"

"You're unbelievable! Do you know that? *No!*"

"But it would be exciting!"

"It would *not* be exciting! It would be nerve-racking, and my nerves are racked enough. What is it with you?"

He playacted pouting. "Spoilsport!"

We reverted to an uneasy silence. I felt like a kettle set to boil, my anxiety bubbling along. The sky above the horizon shifted from pale to royal blue. After a moment I asked, "Would there be any other kind of security?"

"Man dog," replied Brian.

I turned to him. "What?"

"Man dog," he repeated. "That's short for 'a man with a dog.' Usually a Doberman pinscher."

"Doberman pinscher?" I gulped. Don't get me wrong. As I already mentioned, I like dogs. Lassie and Toto? Bring 'em on. Doberman pinschers, on the other hand . . .

"Yeah, I know," Brian said. "I've never liked 'em either. Way too alert for my taste. I like my dogs chill." He glanced at me, then laughed and, reaching over, squeezed my arm. "There won't be any dogs, Randi. We're way out in the country in a place that *is* mostly country. C'mon. Nobody's going to spring for a guy with a dog at a place like this. What's the worst that can happen? Some dweeby junior high schooler takes a Segway for a joyride? Some mini-goths throw a party on the seventh hole? You don't need a dog to break that up."

"Are you sure?"

"Cross my heart and hope to die."

"I don't believe you."

"That's your problem, not mine."

Now the horizon simmered into a thin maroon line, and the sky above it turned deep indigo.

"Besides, Qianfu's ghost is a lot scarier than a Doberman pinscher."

"Shut up!" He just couldn't resist, could he? "Oh, man! Don't talk about that. Not if you want me to be of any use at all."

By the time nine o'clock rolled around it was pitch-dark, and of the dozen or so cars that had been parked in the lot when we arrived only one remained – a battered, white, windowless van. Brian pointed to it. "That'll be security."

At 9:30 sharp the clubhouse went dark, and I mean dark. This far out into the country, with no light pollution coming off a nearby big city and no moon . . . doesn't get much darker than that.

I peered into the gloom. "No security lighting?"

"It costs to burn sodium-vapor lights all night," said Brian. "The lights are probably controlled by some kind of motion detector system around the periphery."

I snorted. "Great! And I suppose the security guy is going to ignore the fact that suddenly the fourth hole is lit up like a Christmas tree?"

"Relax, Randi. He'll assume we're a couple of animals. Nine times out of ten, it's animals that set off motion detectors."

"Animals? Do you mean, like deer?"

"Like deer. Like hedgehogs. Like coyotes."

"Coyotes?"

"And bears."

"*Bears?*"

He checked his watch. "Showtime!"

We'd agreed to wait a few minutes after the clubhouse closed, to let everything settle a little, before downloading the avatar and, you know, heading off into the Valley of the Shadow of Death. But now my mind had snagged on the possibility that there might be bears roaming around. "What kind of bears?" I asked. "Dangerous bears?"

"All bears are potentially dangerous," Brian replied. "Just remember, if we encounter one, stay calm. Don't run. Back away from the bear slowly. Do not look the bear in the eye –"

"Brian!"

"I'm jerking your chain. This country's too open for bears."

I started to relax just a bit . . .

"Besides, Qianfu's ghost is a lot scarier than a bear."

"Brian!"

"Oh, take a pill, why don't you? C'mon. It's the witching hour. Time to get cracking." He rubbed his hands together and I realized that he was excited. It wasn't that he wasn't scared; he was that extra bit hyper, his mania cranked up that couple of extra notches, and I knew he was afraid. After all, he wasn't stupid. But he was psyched too, like this was some crazy adventure. Which I guess it was – but still!

I took a deep, tentative breath. My stomach was tied in some kind of Celtic knot and my chest ached from my efforts not to hyperventilate. This has to be done, I told myself. This has to be done whether I want to do it or not. Even if it's the last thing I do, it has to be done. I sat up straighter, squared my shoulders. "OK," I said, trying to sound resolute. "I'm going to use my GPS to track the grave's coordinates. I don't want to rely on the Zypad for both the GPS and the *feng shui* network in case we lose our connection." With trembling fingers I set the grave's latitude at fifty degrees, twenty-two minutes, and thirty-six seconds north, and its longitude at one hundred and five degrees, forty-one minutes, and four seconds west. Then I muted the audio. Wandering around a pitch-black golf course at night directed by a woman's disembodied voice saying, in a posh British accent, "Follow highlighted route . . . recalculating," didn't seem very smart. Another deep breath. "Now I'm going to download The Grandfather."

"Roger that!"

Using the touch screen, I logged onto the Internet, entered through the New Age portal, selected the *feng shui* network, and did a control find for Liu Xiazong. A moment later, the avatar appeared on the tiny screen and lifted its cane in silent greeting.

I swallowed hard. I looked at Brian. "I guess we're really doing this, huh?"

"Looks like it."

"Give me your I-spex then." He handed me his pair. I charged them with my CanBoard card and handed them back. "Ready to rock?"

"I'm always ready to rock."

We put on the I-spex and powered on.

Again the entry bump, that spinny sense of dislocation, that feeling of being stretched out. I glanced down at the screen of my Zypad, which looked much farther away than it had a moment before. The avatar had vanished. I squinted at the screen. A second later, "Shall we?" – right in my ear. A hot, electric surge of fear ran right through me; it was like being struck by lightning. My heart slammed into reverse and I twisted toward the voice and, sure enough, there was the avatar, hovering outside the car window on my side. It was so close that I could make out the polygonal mesh from which it was modeled – tiny vertices in 3-D space connected by firefly-green lines. I closed my eyes and slumped back into the seat, my hand over my pounding heart. "Oh, man! Don't *do* that."

"Don't do what?"

"Don't just *appear* like that."

"I really don't have any control over how I manifest." The avatar floated through the Helio's back door as though it were not there, which I suppose it wasn't in its whatever it was – dimension? frequency? – and took a seat in midair.

Brian twisted around in his seat to face it. "OK, Gramps, what's our game plan?"

"Gramps?" repeated the avatar, as if it could not possibly have heard him correctly. *"Gramps?"*

"Sorry," Brian apologized hastily. "I mean, Honored Grandfather."

"That's better." The avatar was stern. "An ancestor is owed respect, something you will do well to remember, great-grandson. As for our . . . whatever the sports metaphor was that you used . . ."

"Our game plan."

"Game plan," repeated the avatar. "Ah, yes. Our game plan is very straightforward, Brian. First we must take the precaution of ensuring that the grave in question is indeed that of my brother."

"Yes," I interjected, "and how do we do that, exactly? We can't test for DNA in the field and, besides, wouldn't they have scraped his bones clean in the Death House?"

The avatar regarded me gravely. It shook its head. "If this is my brother, there will be no doubt, Miranda. No doubt whatsoever. All we need to do is disturb the grave to determine the identity of its owner." It turned to Brian. "What have you brought in the way of a body bag?"

"A Pierre Cardin suit bag," replied Brian.

"Good. Good." The avatar nodded its approval. "Qianfu always liked quality." Then its tone turned grave and its mien severe, and it was as though all the oxygen had been sucked out of the car. It spoke in a low voice. "You must understand, great-grandchildren: if Qianfu lies buried here, digging up this grave will be tantamount to knocking down a hornet's nest, only a great deal worse. The ghost will resist with all its might and, as you witnessed yesterday afternoon, its powers are formidable. It is not my dear brother we may encounter tonight, but his hungry ghost. I assure you, it would bear no more resemblance to my poor brother than a hummingbird does to a buzzard. What was human and good in Qianfu has been utterly consumed, leaving behind black rage and darkest malice. That distillation of rage and malice would be our adversary, and a worthy and terrible adversary it –"

Brian interrupted. "Uhhh, excuse me, Honored Grandfather. How exactly would we . . . you know . . . *deal* with the ghost?"

"That would be my job," replied the avatar.

"Yeah, but how would *you* deal with it?"

"Brian!" I pleaded. "Not now!" Brian and his thirst for knowledge! It was beyond irritating.

"It's technical," said the avatar. "You wouldn't understand."

"Try me."

The avatar sighed but, seeing Brian's eager expression, launched into the same kind of explanation it had tried to give me during my disastrous encounter with the giant virtual *lo p'an* back in Calgary. "Well, first I must gather the energy from the Twenty-Four Directions. Then I must enhance and direct it, tapping the energy intrinsic in Earlier Heaven and using it to affect the energy flow and avoid the energy inherent in Later Heaven –"

"Hold on. Whoa." I held up my hand. "Do you see now?" I said, turning to Brian. "Are you satisfied? It's mumbo jumbo."

"I think it's interesting," Brian insisted. "I was listening."

"Well, stop listening and let's get on with this!"

"She's right," the avatar said. "Now is not the time, but I'm glad to see that you are interested. If we make it through this . . . ordeal . . . we shall talk further. Be assured of that."

"I've been thinking," I interjected. "If you're the one who will be dealing with the ghost and Brian's doing all the heavy lifting, what's there for me to do? I mean, I don't mind staying back in the car. I could . . . like . . . keep watch or something."

"Absolutely not." The avatar shook its head. "Your job is essential to this mission. Only a skilled geomancer can deal with a hungry ghost, and I can only do that in this world if you keep me in the picture."

My hope deflated like a balloon some kid stuck a pin in. "So I'm the nerd on site?"

The avatar nodded.

"But what happens if she can't?" Brian asked. "What happens if it is Qianfu and you time out, or she loses the connection?"

The avatar looked very serious indeed. "Well," it said, "then you die."

Ten minutes later, the avatar floating ahead of us like some kind of St. Elmo's fire, we stole across the deserted highway and picked our way through the tangled scrub and weed-choked grass that lined the road to the golf club's parking lot. Brian carried the shovel and hedge clippers, while I carried the suit bag folded over my left arm; the Zypad was fastened tightly around my right arm. Our I-spex bathed the scene as it unfolded before us – the scrub and grass, the gutter of rank-smelling mud that gave the road its ragged edge – in a greenish-golden light. It was a mixed blessing the I-spex conferred: on the one hand, they furnished light and made it possible for us to interact with the avatar; on the other, they seriously messed with our proprioception – our ability to sense exactly where our body parts were in relation to other body parts, or to anything else. The experience was a little like walking down steps in the dark, when you don't know exactly where the next step is. It was way disorienting; it made us both clumsy, and made me dizzy. I don't do dizzy well. I made a mental note to check with Brian on whether he'd kept his barf bag from the virtual tour. I was pretty sure that, before this night was through, I was going to need it. A barf bag or a body bag, one or the other.

We reached the parking lot. Brian cast a covetous eye toward the Segways ranged alongside the clubhouse. "Are you sure you don't want me to steal a couple?"

I couldn't believe he was still on about that. "Are you nuts?"

"It would make for a faster getaway."

"If you do that, I'll have a heart attack. I'm already as nervous as a cat."

"That's because you drank all that Fizz at dinner. I told you to take it easy."

"No Segways, Brian." The avatar's tone was firm. "It's too risky. And no dawdling. The longer this takes us, the more likely it is we'll lose our connection. Miranda, lead the way."

"Why don't you lead the way?"

"Because I don't know where I'm going. I'm a virtual entity, not omniscient. It's up to you to take us to the grave."

"But I've only been here once," I objected. "In daylight."

"You've got the grave's coordinates dialed into your GPS," Brian reminded me.

"Oh, right." I checked our coordinates. "This way." I led

them around the outside of the parking lot, in the direction of the first hole.

I was struck by how very different the course looked at night – drained of color, and teeming with elongated shadows that swayed and loomed in the slight breeze. And it was noisy – I could distinguish cricket chirps and owl hoots and frog croaks, along with scurrying sounds and the whisper of something running softly through the wheat. What *was* that? A hedgehog? A coyote? How big were coyotes? Did they attack humans? I shivered in my CanBoard hoodie. It was chilly for August, but then this was Saskatchewan.

"Check those out, why don't you?" Brian pointed toward the sky.

I tilted my head back and gazed into a thick carpet of twinkling stars stretching overhead as far as the eye could see. "Wow."

"Ah, yes," said the avatar. "I had forgotten how many stars are visible here, how clear the night skies are. Not like Vancouver."

"See that flare?" I pointed at a light streaking across the sky. "That's a satellite pass."

The avatar shook its head. "The sky is cluttered with so many things nowadays." It sighed. "When I was a boy, there were only the stars."

"If it weren't for satellites, there would be no satellite Internet or radio or TV," I pointed out. "No GPS. Speaking of which . . ." I checked back in with the GPS. "This way," I said, and picked my way down the gentle slope of the hole and past the inky ponds that flanked it, followed by Brian; the avatar took up the rear. Once again I consulted the GPS, then headed down the cart path, around a copse of cedars to the second hole, and along the edge of the pond to which I had consigned so many balls earlier that day. In the midst of all this, it occurred to me that I might have to pee sometime soon. Great, I thought. Just what I need.

The third hole, zigzagging one way, then the other, then back again, was like an obstacle course. The avatar floated effortlessly over the mounds and bunkers, but Brian and I had to walk around or clamber over every landform and, remember, there was that little problem of proprioception. I stumbled like a drunk and timbered twice, landing once on my backside with a wicked jolt, and once on my knees, ripping my jeans. Brian was more coordinated, but he still managed to trip a couple of times, catching himself just short of falling. But the worst thing was that I was now convinced I had to pee. *Soon.*

We reached the fourth hole.

"This is it!" Brian was saying. "The fourth hole. Where the grave is." He pointed to the eruption of earth crowned with bushes.

"The fourth hole?" the avatar asked. "The fourth, you say?" It shook its head. "So unlucky!"

Brian elbowed me in the ribs. "See? I told you. The number four is unlucky."

"Not to mention *that* abomination." The avatar pointed to the porta-potty. It had been shrouded in darkness at the edge of the green, but now that we turned our I-spex in its direction, it shone the same neon blue that pool bottoms are painted.

"The porta-potty!" How could I have forgotten? I was saved. "Thank heavens!"

The other two turned to look at me.

"I have to pee."

"Now?"

"Yes, now!"

"I told you not to drink so much," said Brian, sounding exasperated. "You know you have a bladder the size of a pea."

"Don't say 'pea.'"

"Well, go on then," he said.

"But I *hate* porta-potties." I had only used a porta-potty once, when I was a child at some park. I could still remember the strong odor of disinfectant barely masking the other smells, the gaping dark hole down which I dared not look, and, worst of all, the feeling that the molded plastic walls were closing in around me.

"So pee outside."

"Outside? Like a dog?"

"It's not going to kill you. Go over there. Behind that tree."

"But, Brian –"

"*Honestly*, Randi!" He dropped the shovel and headed toward the berry bushes, hedge clippers in hand.

"When I first came to Chinatown in Vancouver, men would come around every morning to collect the contents of privies, which they would then use to fertilize their gardens," recollected the avatar. "These men were called night-soil men. Those were good times."

"Uggh. You are *so* not helping!" I steeled myself. People used porta-potties all the time and nothing bad happened to them. Besides, this was a fancy golf course; no well-heeled business dude was going to put up with some crappy porta-potty. Smarten up, I told myself.

I laid the suit bag down next to the shovel, rummaged in my knapsack for my industrial hand wipes, removed one, and forced myself to walk over to the structure. Taking a deep breath, I reached out and opened the door with the wipe. A faint odor seeped out. Not too bad, I told myself. But the enclosure was narrow – only three feet square – and I tend to get claustrophobic under pressure. Please don't let me have a panic attack, I prayed. Please! I stepped up into the porta-potty and pulled the door shut, again using the wipe. I pulled down my ripped jeans and lowered myself gingerly over the toilet seat, being careful not to let my skin touch the plastic. I didn't want to think what germs might be on that seat. Dangerous germs in lurid shades of green and purple, with wiggly edges and malicious grins, as seen in Lysol, Mr. Clean, Chlorox, and Cepacol commercials. What can I say? I'm highly impressionable.

A moment later, as I was relieving myself of the three cans of Guarana Fizz with which I had washed down supper, I heard a loud, high-pitched wailing sound.

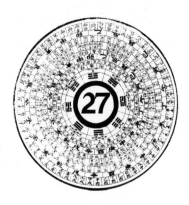

Beep! Beep! Beep!

Yanking my jeans up around my hips, I struggled to my feet. "What is it? What's going on?"

Brian's response was barely audible over the alarm's high-pitched beeping: "Must . . . laser security," was all I could make out. That and "Beam . . . broken." Great. The perimeter of the grave was protected by a laser beam, and Cousin Doofus had just broken it!

"I'm coming!" I shot back. "Hold on!" Like I was the cavalry or Mighty Mouse: Here I come to save the day! There was just one problem. When I tried the door handle, it refused to turn. I stared at it with disbelief. Had I locked it? I shook my head. I hadn't locked it; I'd only latched it, I was sure. I rattled the handle, then tugged on it. I pushed it as far to the left as I could, then to the right. *Nada.* My heart pounded in my chest.

This was *so* not good. The alarm sounded like a fanfare for Armageddon; meanwhile, I'm trapped in a porta-potty. "Brian!" I yelled. "The door's locked! I can't get out!"

"The door's locked?" Brian's voice, nearby now. He must have left the stand of bushes and come down to where I was. "You locked it? Did you think I was going to burst in on you?"

"No! I don't know! I didn't lock it!"

"What?"

"I didn't lock it!"

"Maybe it's just stuck."

I ground the heels of my hands into my ears to blot out the sound of the alarm. "That alarm is driving me *crazy!*" I wailed. "*Do* something!"

"Do what?"

"Get me out of here!"

And that's when I heard it – or rather *felt* it, because at first it was more a vibration than a sound. And it grew and grew. It grew until it drowned out even the shrill honk of the alarm. It grew until it was so all-encompassing, so huge, that nothing but it and I seemed to exist, with me a mere speck compared to the swirling, howling, raging vortex of sound – equal parts wrenching despair and towering rage, as if the space-time continuum were being ripped from its bearings, as if the universe were collapsing into itself. The noise was so vast, so horrendous, that it was a few moments before it dawned on me that the sound, the vibration, the . . . whatever it was came not from the real world but from the virtual one. I fumbled frantically with the controls on the side of my I-spex and finally managed to find the off switch for the earphones.

And then it was gone, all of it – the alarm too. My head spun; my knees sagged; my ears rang hollowly as though I were at the bottom of a well. What the . . . ?

A sharp rap against the outside of the porta-potty. Brian.

"Brian, turn off your earphones," I cried. "The off switch is on the side of your I-spex!"

"What?"

"The off switch! For your earphones."

"My earphones *are* off."

"So you didn't hear . . . ?"

"Didn't hear what? I heard the alarm, all right! My ears are still ringing."

"No, not the alarm. The other. Really loud . . ." I paused. Whatever had just happened to me, whatever I had just experienced . . . there were no words to describe it, not that I could think of, anyway. And coming up with a reasonable explanation wasn't going to get me out of that porta-potty, which, in my books, was job *numero uno*. "Never mind! Just get me out of here."

And that was when I felt it, felt it for real. The floor of the porta-potty began to quiver, then to quake. The toilet seat started jittering. I clapped my hand over my mouth and stared at the seat with horror. "Omigod!" I gasped.

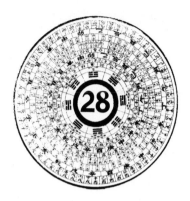

O"migod *what?*" Brian's voice, sharp with urgency.

"There's something down there!"

"Down where?"

"In the toilet!"

"Quick, put down the lid and sit on it."

"What?"

"You heard me!"

I flung down the lid and sat down on it hard; it danced underneath me like the lid of a boiling kettle.

"Brace yourself!"

"Brace myself? How?" I searched the molded plastic walls to either side of me – there was nowhere to hold onto, nothing to grip. "Why?"

"I'm going to tip you!"

"Tip me?"

"I'm going to tip the porta-potty! It's the only way."

"Brian, no!"

I felt the porta-potty lurch from right to left. "Whoa!" In a panic, I planted my feet on the door in front of me and pushed against it with all my might. Even so, it was all I could do to keep my bum pressing down on the seat. Then the porta-potty lurched right again, at a much sharper angle this time. It hung in midair for one heart-stopping moment, then crashed to the ground with a resounding thud. The impact caused the jammed door to burst open, and sent me sliding off the seat, over the door's sill, and onto the grass, feet first. Brian stood over me, laughing. "Look what you did! I told you not to drink so much Fizz. You broke the toilet!"

"Shut up!" I snapped. "It wasn't my fault! There's something seriously wrong with that toilet!" I held out my hands. "Help me up!" He grabbed me by my wrists and hauled me to my feet.

"Brian! Miranda!" The avatar pointed toward the downed porta-potty with the green globe of its cane. We looked back in that direction, and Brian quickly wrapped his arm around my waist and pulled me aside. Just in time, as it turned out. The jittering lid flew open and an evil-looking and foul-smelling liquid started to ooze over the lip of the toilet.

"What the . . . ?"

But it wasn't just the tank's foul contents oozing out of

the toilet. There was something else as well. Something beginning to thicken and congeal, beginning to take shape.

Suddenly the toilet lid began to chatter maniacally. It reminded me of this stupid joke toy my dad used to bring out at parties, a set of teeth that you wound up and they would chatter and lurch drunkenly around a tabletop. Only that was kind of funny, and this really wasn't.

And then it got worse.

Poisonous green smoke started steaming from the hole.

"I'd say we found our man," Brian said quietly. "Just like the Mounties."

"No shit, Sherlock!" I managed to croak.

"It's time," the avatar said quietly. "Brian, Miranda, it's time." But we just stood there, dumbfounded and staring. All the smoke and ooze were melding together into something that was becoming three-dimensional . . . I don't know how to describe it. It was compelling. It was hypnotic. "Don't look at him," the avatar warned us. "He'll gain power over you if you look at him." But it was as if its voice came from far away.

"Him?" I repeated dreamily. "Who's 'him'?"

"Qianfu! Miranda, Brian! Look away, I tell you!"

Then the shape did something that got our attention – a real showstopper. It exploded, and green globs flew everywhere. Instantly, the spell was broken.

I wheeled to face Brian. "What . . . ? Where'd it go?"

"I don't know!"

Then the avatar's disembodied voice: "Give me the *lo p'an*, Miranda. *Now.*"

I looked this way and that. "What? How? Where are you?"

The myriad of green globs began to act like one of those schools of fish that elude predators by dazzling them. You know what I mean – the fish go this way, then that, moving as a unit, compressing and expanding and making all kinds of crazy shapes, and it all seems to be choreographed, only how could that be? They're *fish*. And then, *bam*, a flash expansion and suddenly gone, and in its place the avatar, only much bigger than before – seven, maybe even nine feet tall.

"That's a neat trick," said Brian.

"I'll teach you how to do it one day," the avatar replied. "If you survive this. The *lo p'an*, Miranda! *Miranda!*"

"Just a sec. I know it was here somewhere . . ." I rooted in my knapsack.

"Give it here!" Snatching the knapsack from me, Brian retrieved the cherrywood box from its side pocket, opened it, removed the *lo p'an*, and lobbed it to the avatar. The compass tumbled end over end through the air as it described the now familiar arc that began in our world and ended in the avatar's. It paused at the arc's midpoint for a mere second, suspended, before executing a spin so fast that all we saw was a blur. Then, with a wet-sounding *pop*, it penetrated the membrane that stretched between our two realities, actual and virtual. The avatar caught it with both hands and turned to face the downed porta-potty.

"Get out of here," it ordered. "Both of you. Dig him up. Do it as quickly as you can."

Something turned over in my brain, clicking into place like a gear shifting, then locking. I grabbed the suit bag. "Someone's bound to have heard that alarm," I told Brian. "We've got to hurry."

"Right!" He turned abruptly and started across the tee, with me on his heels. As we crouched to step through the ragged opening he had cut in the wall of the berry bush, I had to suppress an urge to look back over my shoulder. Don't, I told myself grimly. That way madness lies. There's only one way now, and that's forward.

The instant I stepped through the breach in the bushes and into the clearing, my Zypad went off with a shriek.

"What's the matter?" Brian hissed. "Why's it doing that?"

"It's detecting that bloody laser beam you broke," I snapped. That kind of frantic *beep-beep-beep* is annoying when you're chill; when you're not chill, it's enough to send you through the roof. "It picks up invisible info: sensor data, radiation levels, lines of force . . .".

"Never mind that! Can't you disarm it?"

"I'm doing that, Brian! Just give me a sec. We don't want to trip that laser beam again." I consulted the Zypad, made some adjustments, and zoomed in. "OK," I said, "according to this, the beam is about two feet into the enclosure and around three feet high. I see just the one beam and it looks to be static, not oscillating, so we should be OK to crawl under it." Crushing the suit bag to my chest, I dropped to my hands and knees and crawled under the beam. Brian followed suit. Three feet inside the perimeter I consulted the Zypad again. "All clear."

I stood and glanced around. The space within the bushes was larger than it had looked from outside, certainly larger than I had expected, maybe fifteen feet by fifteen. Its center was marked by a slab of granite, rough on one side, polished on the other, to which a bronze plaque had been affixed. I crossed over to it and crouched down. "'Here lie the remains of an unknown First Nations man believed to have been an ancestor of the Stoney Sioux of this region,'" I read. I stood and glanced around me. "But where is 'here'? We don't have time to dig up this entire space. This is a job for IAF."

"IAF?"

"Infrastructural anatomy function – a walk-on-map function. It lets me see underground. I'm going down." I switched on the function and gazed down at the ground through the quivering yellow grid that the application had superimposed over my field of vision. "Elijah said it was a shallow grave, didn't he?"

"Two feet."

"I'm going to set the maximum at three feet, then. We

can go deeper if we need to." I adjusted the controls and began to slowly walk the grid, keeping my eyes fixed on the ground as the function drilled down one foot, then two, until suddenly a glowing lime-green 3-D shape reminiscent of a mummy appeared on the screen.

It was the symbol used by WorldBoard to designate a burial.

I stopped in my tracks and pointed wordlessly at the ground.

There it was. There *he* was, what was left of him. Qianfu, The Grandfather's twin brother. What we had come here for, what had eluded us all this time. And by "us" I meant not just Brian and me, but all of those who had borne the name Liu over many years. Qianfu was unlucky in life, unlucky in love, and the hapless victim of a hate crime whose repercussions had extended far beyond his murder and down through the generations until finally, *finally,* what had been for so long lost was found. I turned to look at Brian, my eyes wide, and held out my arm so that he could see the Zypad's screen.

"Wow," he said, and we both stared at the ground, speechless, for the moment at least.

I roused myself to action. After all, how much time did we have before somebody responded to that alarm? It couldn't be long now. "Follow this line," I told Brian. Using the toe of my Keds, I traced the outline of the grave as it appeared on my grid. Brian followed close behind me, deepening the outline with the shovel's blade. The surface area of the grave was quite small, maybe three feet by three feet – smaller than a typical grave, presumably because it contained loose bones rather than a complete skeleton. Government policy dictated that First Nations burial sites be left undisturbed; that had worked to our advantage. Had the bones been removed from the site, they would have probably been placed in some kind of ossuary and reburied in a standard seven-foot-deep grave, not Rawlins's shallow two-foot one. A deeper grave would have required a much greater effort, and far more time to dig up. We were lucky – if catching a break after generations of being cursed could be considered lucky.

While Brian cut the sod above the grave, I retrieved the suit bag, laid it on the ground, and unzipped it. Then I straightened up and, hugging myself tightly and chewing on my lower lip, looked on as Brian methodically sliced the sod into squares with the shovel's blade end. Too methodically, for my taste. Who cared how neat a job he did? "What are you doing?" I demanded. "Why aren't you digging?"

"I'm the landscape guy, remember? I know what I'm doing. *First* you lift the sod. *Then* you dig."

"I don't like this," I fretted. "I can't believe nobody's going to check out that alarm." I glanced over my shoulder toward the opening in the bushes. "And it's way too quiet. What's going on out there, anyway? With The Grandfather and the ghost? Why don't we *hear* anything?"

"Do you want me to dig or listen?"

"Dig!"

And that was when we heard it – a distant combination of growl and bark, coming from the direction of the clubhouse. All the hairs on my neck stood on end, and my stomach lurched.

"Uh-oh," said Brian.

"You told me that there wouldn't be any dogs!"

"I told you there *probably* wouldn't be any dogs."

"You sounded awfully positive!"

"I'm a positive kind of guy!"

I wrung my hands. "That doesn't sound like a nice dog!"

"No, it really doesn't. On the bright side, it sounds like there's only one of them."

"Great!"

I took a deep breath, closed my eyes, and gave myself a stern talking-to: OK, Miranda, if it's a choice between being mauled by a dog now or eaten by a shark later, then . . . then what? I snorted. Who was I kidding? The only *real* choice I had was how I was going to handle this challenge, whether I was going to be paralyzed with fear or go down fighting. And I *could* choose. I couldn't always choose what happened to me – I often couldn't, and I certainly hadn't chosen this whole Qianfu thing – but I sure as heck could choose how I dealt with it. "Oh well, maybe he'll only maul us a little," I said to Brian. "You keep digging. I'll suss the dog thing out." Making my way to the edge of the clearing, I dropped to my hands and knees, crawled under the laser beam, and crouched in the opening.

What I saw took my breath away, as surely as though someone had punched me hard in the stomach. I sat back on my heels and stared, jaw slack with amazement.

The felled porta-potty lay in a pool of some dark, lustrous substance that gleamed like liquid mercury and seemed to have similar properties. The ancients called mercury "quicksilver," meaning "living silver," but the disgusting pool from the porta-potty, whatever it was, was not silver but poisonous green. A form rose from the pool like a stalagmite from the floor of a cave, glistening and slippery. At first I thought it was composed of the same matter as the pool, but then I realized that there was someone or, more likely, some*thing* encased within the green ooze, something that was trying to free itself.

Could that be Qianfu's hungry ghost? I could just make out a pitifully tiny mouth, wide open in a soundless scream, and two eyes like burning embers that radiated hatred and despair. Hatred and despair – a toxic combination, an altogether more potent concoction than hatred alone. After all, despair fuels hatred, and despair has nothing more to lose. And what is a more terrifying enemy than one with nothing to lose? Oh, surely it was Qianfu! Who or what else could it be?

I leaned forward to try to get a better look. That was when I noticed the membrane – a thick, transparent membrane like that of a jellyfish, wrapped tight around the struggling form. It seemed to have a life of its own; it pulsated rhythmically, like a heart. It struck me that it was this and this alone that prevented Qianfu's ghost from breaking free. Where had it come from?

I glanced to my left and found my answer: the avatar. The membrane was like some kind of magical net that it had cast over the ghost, a force field of some sort, and now they were locked in this wicked cosmic standoff. The avatar stood facing the ghost, supersized. It loomed, arms outstretched, with the glowing green globe in one hand and the *lo p'an* in the other.

All of a sudden, I heard a man's voice and heavy canine panting and, I swear it, slavering. How could I have forgotten? The savage dog, the security guard . . . reality check! My heart skittered like a stone over water, slammed into something hard, and went into a death spiral. I dropped to my belly like a snake and wriggled backward, far enough into the bushes that I could see and not be seen – unless the security guard were to shine a flashlight in my direction, in which case it would be well and truly *game over*.

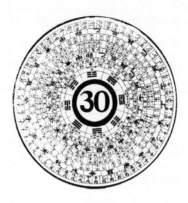

"Damn kids," I heard. "Nah, they've just overturned the porta-potty. The fourth hole. Yeah. What a mess! One thing I can tell you, Bob, glad it's not me who has to clean it up! Wouldn't want to be a maintenance guy tomorrow morning!"

What would we be charged with? I lay there on my belly, with brambles poking in my face, thinking hard. Trespassing, probably. Vandalism, obviously. But trespassing and vandalism weren't so bad. We were teenagers, after all, and that is what teenagers do – go places they aren't supposed to and break a bunch of stuff. Normal teenagers, that is, unlike us, two Asian kids from out of province whose elders, living and dead, have sent them on a mission to lift the family curse by digging up a supposedly First Nations burial site and hauling the ancient bones back to B.C. This was not normal; it was *weird*. Maybe telling the truth wasn't so smart. How serious a crime was desecrating a grave, anyway? Would we get off easy, with community service, or would we have to go to some kind of jail? That we would get caught I didn't doubt. It was only a question of time. I mean, what kind of nimrod security guard would *not* notice a person-sized hole cut in the bushes?

At that very moment, the guard was telling good old Bob, "What I can't figure out is how they broke that beam."

OK, I thought, here it comes.

"These bushes look pretty impenetrable . . ."

Brace yourself, Miranda. Any second now . . .

There was a silence, then "Pooky!" The guard sounded surprised.

Pooky? Who was Pooky?

"What is it, girl? What's the matter?"

Of course! It was the dog he was talking to. Pooky the killing machine. Pooky, whose reply was a high-pitched yelp followed by a whimper — much to my surprise and relief.

I crept forward a little and peered out. There was the security guard, standing with his back to the mess, a sleek, pointy-eared Doberman cowering at his side. The guard was bulky and bald and had a headset hooked over one ear; he was training a big industrial flashlight on the felled porta-potty. For a second I couldn't believe my eyes. He was looking straight at, and apparently straight *through*, The Grandfather and Qianfu's hungry ghost. How could he not see them? They were so . . . right in front of him! Then I realized that I could only see them – The Grandfather, at any rate – because of the I-spex. How I would experience the ghost in a non-virtual state, I had no way of knowing. None of this explained why Pooky could see them. Because it was pretty clear from her posture and her manner that she did see them, or at least sensed them.

"Hey, Pookster," the guard said. Suddenly he appeared uncertain, even uneasy. "What's with you, anyway?" Once again the dog yelped and slunk behind him, tail between her legs, shivering. "Beats the heck out of me, Bob." He sounded worried now. "She's scared of something, all right. Real scared." He glanced around, shining his flashlight here and there, but in front of him, around the porta-potty, not back in our direction. "Tell you the truth, Bobby, this is making me kind of nervous. If the dog is freaked out . . . you know, they don't pay me enough that it's worth . . ." He let out an anxious "whew," and swallowed hard. "Well, whoever done this is probably long gone. I'll file the report with maintenance. They can check on it in the morning." Then, to Pooky, "OK, OK, we're going. Calm down, would you?"

I managed to sneak a peek around the edge of the hole cut in the brambles just long enough to get a look at Pooky's face as she dragged the guard off in the direction of the clubhouse, straining at her leash. I've never in my life seen a dog so terrified.

Somebody touched my shoulder lightly. It was Brian. "What happened?" he whispered.

"They're gone," I whispered back. "The dog could see them – The Grandfather and the ghost. The guy couldn't, but the dog definitely could. She was scared, and that scared him. They won't come back. We're in the clear."

Brian whistled softly. "Crazy! Maybe it's like those animals that make it to higher ground when a tsunami strikes. Somehow they just know it's coming. They feel it in their bones. Speaking of which . . . guess who I've found?"

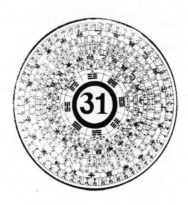

A moment later, I was kneeling beside the grave and peering into the shallow hole at a jumble of soil-stained bones piled up in its approximate center. To one side of the pile lay a grubby-looking skull, to the other a pelvic bone. "We really didn't need a suit bag, did we?" I said. "A good-sized tote would have done the trick."

"Do the honors?" Brian offered.

I shuddered. "Are you kidding? *Eeuw!*"

Brian snorted. "What a squeamer!" Lying on his stomach, he reached into the grave and brought up Qianfu's skull. The soil had stained it ocher in places, with patches of green that looked suspiciously like mold. He pointed to a jagged break beginning just over the hole where Qianfu's left eye had been. "Old hockey injury?"

I held the suit bag open and looked away so I wouldn't

have to see the skull up close. "Duh! He was beaten, Doofus. That's how he died."

"At least he kept all his teeth." Brian deposited the skull inside the bag. "Although, I gotta say, they could use a good brushing." Reaching back into the grave, he retrieved the pelvic bone. "Sorry for manhandling your privates, dude," he apologized to the bones. He glanced in the direction of the tee and the porta-potty. "What the heck is going on out there, anyway?"

Where to start? "Do you remember that stinky ooze that came out of the porta-potty?"

"Yeah?"

"Turned out to be Qianfu's ghost, or at least some of it was. It's hard to tell what's exactly what. It's all kind of . . . commingled."

"You're kidding me!" Brian was pulling out bones and placing them randomly in the bag. Fibulas? Tibias?

"And now . . . now The Grandfather and the ghost are locked in . . . I don't know what they're locked in. Some kind of slo-mo cosmic smackdown's the best way I can describe it. Not a whole lot is going on, but it looks super weird."

"Whaddya mean?" Brian surfaced with what had to be a scapula.

"The Grandfather has the ghost all wrapped in some bizarre transparent gel or force field or something."

"Get out of here! Force field? What the heck are these, anyway?"

"Phalanges," I identified the bunch of small bones he held out to me. "Fingers."

"Wicked! I have a handful of fingers!"

"Or toes."

"A cosmic smackdown . . ." Brian rose up on his haunches and looked toward the opening cut in the bush. "I'm sorry, cuz, but this I gotta see."

I had just reached out to restrain him when these two ginormous forms heaved into sight, above the bushes, silhouetted against the night sky. Both The Grandfather and the ghost had shot up to twice their already supersized height, so they were now as tall as a two-story building and towering over us. Needless to say, it was pretty startling. I gave a strangled little scream and toppled backward onto my bum, and Brian froze.

The ghost now appeared to be entirely confined within the jelly-like membrane, which had thickened and grown more opaque than when I had last seen it. This had the effect of further squashing the ghost, rendering its few features indistinct – its glittering red eyes were now pinkish smudges, and its gaping mouth a gray blur.

"How are you two doing, anyway?" The Grandfather asked, without looking away from the ghost.

"Uh, fine!" I managed.

"Almost finished!" croaked Brian.

"Well, make it snappy. This isn't exactly easy."

"Right!" Brian fell back onto his knees and began to pull bones out of the grave with both hands, fast, like a dog digging a hole. I saw a femur fly past, and a sternum attached to a rib cage, and what might have been a clavicle.

"Uh . . . what exactly are you doing?" I asked the avatar.

"Isn't it obvious? I'm using the *lo p'an* to trap this evil spirit and bind it to me."

"There," gasped Brian, panting with the effort. "That's all of them. The bones, that is."

"Shouldn't we count them?" I worried. "Make sure he's got two of everything he should have two of, and all his fingers and toes?"

"Not necessary," replied the avatar. "He doesn't need all his bones, just most of them. Your job here is done. Now you must get his bones to Vancouver as quickly as possible, and bury them in the spot reserved for him. Your grandmother will have prepared your mother for this. Daisy will know what to do."

Brian sprang to his feet and brushed himself off. He had grass stains on his knees, and his hands and arms were stained with soil. His face, where he wiped the sweat away, was streaked with dirt. He reached for the shovel.

"Leave it," ordered The Grandfather. "The clippers too. They'll just slow you down."

"But they're evidence!" I protested. "They've got Brian's fingerprints all over them. Mine too."

"Your wipes!" said Brian. "Those things you haul around in your knapsack. Wouldn't they clean off fingerprints?"

My industrial wipes! "You're right! They're perfect!" I dug around in my knapsack, surfaced with the pack, and handed Brian a couple of towelettes. Then I peeled off a couple for myself and went to work on the clipper handles, while he wiped down the shovel. We set the gardening tools side by side to the right of the grave, being careful not to touch them with our fingers.

"Go now," said the avatar. "Quickly."

"But what about you?" Brian asked.

"My work is only beginning."

"But what about maintaining the connection to the Web? You said that was critical."

"Critical to the first phase of the operation," replied the avatar. "To trapping and binding this evil spirit to me. For that a *lo p'an* is required, a *real* one. As none was available in cyberspace, I was compelled to call upon you to bring it to me. Now its work is done, and I must restore it to its proper reality, to the human realm. Brian?"

"What?"

"Catch!"

The avatar tossed the *lo p'an* lightly to him. The familiar arc, the contrail of tiny star shapes, then – *pop* – what had centuries before been an elephant's tusk crafted into something magical flowered into three dimensions and tumbled through the air. Brian deftly caught it, backhanded, like a baseball.

"It's yours now," the avatar told him.

"Really?" Brian looked awed. "Wow! Thanks!"

"Hey!" I objected. "A-Ma gave the compass to me!"

"For safekeeping only," the avatar reminded me. "You have many gifts, Miranda, and they will serve you well in life. But you aren't the one destined to follow in my footsteps. Brian is."

I could scarcely believe my ears. *"Brian?"*

"For centuries a Liu has been a great geomancer. It is Brian's karma to take up that mantle."

"But I can't read," Brian protested. "How can I take it over from you if I can't read? Are you saying that I'll be able to read once the curse is lifted?"

"Your dyslexia is not your curse," the avatar said, "any more than Miranda's germaphobia is her curse. It's just the way you happen to be wired – for better or for worse. Your dyslexia has made you more compassionate, Brian, more understanding and a more creative problem solver than you would have otherwise been. Miranda's germaphobia has made her more . . . well . . . clean."

"Thanks a million," I grumbled.

"Then what is my curse?" Brian demanded.

"If you really must know, you are to be eaten by a shark."

"Wait a minute," I protested. "That's my curse!"

"Brian is to be eaten by a shark off the coast of Bermuda

while trying to rescue you," the avatar said pointedly. "And that's exactly what is going to happen if the two of you don't get out of here right this minute and let me finish what we've started. Now, go. I mean it."

"But what's the second phase?" Brian insisted. "You said the first phase was trapping and binding the ghost. What's the second phase?"

"If you really must know, it's *tai chi*," replied the avatar, sounding a little sheepish. "Do you always ask so many questions?"

"*Tai chi?*" Brian repeated. "That thing old Chinese people do in the park?"

"*Ai ya!* Did you children learn *nothing* in Chinese school?" The Grandfather sounded exasperated. "*Tai chi* is an ancient and profound spiritual practice. Didn't your A-Ma tell you that I was a student of the school of *tai chi* developed by the revered Taoist Zhang Sanfeng, whose graceful movements were as smooth as a reflection in a mirror and whose turns were as natural as pulling silk? Who was so powerful that he was easily able to banish ghosts and other evil spirits?"

"Uh, no," said Brian doubtfully. "I think I would have remembered that."

"Enough! Now is not the time. Off-line, both of you!"

"Are you sure?" I asked.

"*Power off, Miranda!*"

"But if we turn off our I-spex, how will we be able to see?" I cried. "They're our only light source."

"Trust me," the avatar said grimly. "There will be plenty of light. Off! *Now!*"

I gulped, then turned to Brian. "Ready?"

"Ready!"

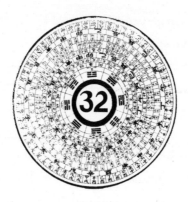

My finger pressed the off button at the side of the I-spex and there it was again – that intense sensation skydivers must feel when they step out of a plane and into the ether and they're falling, falling, falling faster than they can think. Only it's not like falling so much as being sucked toward the earth at the same time it rushes up to meet you.

Of course, some people *like* that feeling – that heart-about-to-burst, stomach-jammed-up-your throat sensation. They crave it. Do crazy things to get their fix of it. Bungee jumping off high bridges and roller-coaster rides. People like Brian. Not people like me.

A reassuring click and there I was, back in the human realm, standing on the fourth hole of Weeping Birches Golf Course under a navy blue sky packed with stars, a suit bag stuffed with bones at my feet.

"Wow," Brian gasped. "That's what I call a rush."

"I don't know," I said, peeling off my I-spex and rubbing my eyes. "I must be allergic to adrenaline. I feel sick." I glanced around. No avatar, no ghost. And it was bloody dark all of a sudden. I squinted at the space they had occupied moments before, trying to conjure them. Not a trace. Yet I knew they were there. In some other reality, on some other plane of existence, but there, and the outcome of their struggle would determine my fate and Brian's and that of my entire family. It was nerve-racking to think about. So don't think about it, I told myself. You have a job to do. *Focus.*

As for the tipped porta-potty, it was indisputably of this world, as were the foul contents of its tank, no longer a gleaming green pool but a mucky, stinking brown ooze. My stomach flopped over and my nose crinkled. "Let's get out of here before I barf!" I tested the suit bag's heft. Twenty pounds of shifting bones, jutting this way and that through the thin fabric.

"Gimme that," Brian offered. "It looks like it's getting away from you." He replaced the *lo p'an* carefully in its case, crammed it into a vest pocket, and reached for the bag. "Man, it's dark. Wonder what The Grandfather meant when he said we'd have plenty of light."

I pointed toward the horizon, which glowed a faint red. "Maybe he meant that."

"I don't get it," said Brian. "It's way too early for sunrise. Is that east?"

I shook my head. "North. Hey!"

Immense curtains of color – blues and greens and red and pink and violet and orange – began to ripple across the night sky in an east-west direction, one graceful arc blending into the next.

"What the . . . ?"

I put my hand on his arm. "The aurora borealis. I've never seen it before."

"Me neither. You don't think . . . ?"

"Think what?"

"That this is . . . well, you know."

I gazed at the sky, filled with wonder. It was profoundly beautiful, the most beautiful sight I had ever seen. "Technically speaking, the aurora borealis is nothing more than the inter-action between the earth's magnetic field and solar wind."

"Technically speaking."

"*Un*technically speaking, however . . ."

We looked at one another.

"Untechnically speaking, I'd say The Grandfather is practicing *tai chi*."

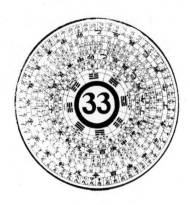

33

We had not gone three miles down the deserted high-way from the golf club when we spotted a solitary light wobbling toward us from the direction of Moose Jaw. "What the . . . ? Is that a *bike*? On the highway? You're kidding me!" Brian switched to low beam and shifted forward in his seat to scan the road unfolding in front of the Helio. Overhead, the aurora still performed its diaphanous dance of many veils; curtains of color rippled across the sky as far as the eye could see. "It *is* a bike!" he concluded.

"At this time of night?" I leaned forward and squinted at the road ahead. "Omigod. Brian! I think it's *Elijah*!"

"Elijah who?"

"Elijah what's-his-name. The homeless guy."

"Elijah *Otter*?" Abruptly Brian turned the wheel and pulled over to the shoulder. He stopped the car and rolled down his window. The rider wove uncertainly into view – an ungainly man, tall, stooped, and skeletal. He was wearing a windbreaker, baggy khakis, and a toque.

"Hey, Elijah!"

The rider braked about ten feet from the car. He shielded his eyes and peered in our direction. "Who wants to know?"

"It's Brian. Brian and Miranda. From the hotel."

Elijah's face exploded into a big, gap-toothed grin that made the corners of his heavy-lidded eyes crinkle up; he looked like one of those goofy jack-o'-lanterns. "Oh, yeah," he said, stepping carefully off the bike and walking it alongside the car. "Hi there."

"You're riding a bike!"

"I am," replied Elijah. He shook his head. "They say you never forget how. I'm not so sure about that."

"When did you get a bike?"

Elijah looked a little sheepish. He scratched his cheek with jagged, dirty fingernails. "That money you gave me. I was going to use it for booze, but then . . ." He shrugged. "Then I thought, that's what they think I'll use it for, and I'm tired of people being right about me. I bought this bike instead."

His words made my heart hurt. I closed my eyes and shrank back into the bucket seat. Why do I always think the worst of people? Why do I do that? The truth is, I'm not a very nice person. I'm going to try to be better, I promised myself, to not be so quick to judge.

"Good for you," Brian congratulated him.

"I thought about what you said, man. That I should go back to where I come from, leave the city behind. There's been nothing but bad for me in Moose Jaw. So, you know, that's what I'm doing. I'm going home to Old Wives Lake."

"On a bike?" Brian asked. "Isn't that, like, twenty miles?"

Elijah grinned again. "Hey, man, you only gave me three hundred dollars. If you'd given me more, I'd a bought a car."

Brian laughed. "But where's Lois?"

Elijah pointed to a fluorescent orange child trailer attached to the back of the bike. A plaintive yelp leaked out of it. "She's pretty freaked out," he said, "but I keep telling her things are going to be just fine."

"Are you sure you wouldn't like a ride?"

"Brian!" I tugged at his elbow. I was going to be a better person, I was, but not until we got Qianfu's bones laid safely to rest and I wasn't going to be eaten by a shark off Bermuda. "We're in kind of a hurry. Remember?"

"But it's only –"

"Nah." Elijah shook his head and indicated the sky with a sweep of his hand. "Don't you see what a beautiful night it is? You see the Northern Lights a lot in these parts, but I've never seen them like this. Nope, not like this. It's just . . . *majestic* is what it is. You know what my people call the northern lights?"

"No," said Brian. "What?"

"Dancing Spirits. They are the spirits of our ancestors.

They don't want us to forget them, so they dance in the sky to remind us that they once lived and loved like us, and that one day we too will dance in the sky for all our descendants to see."

"My people have a similar theory," said Brian. "We think the aurora is our ancestors using *tai chi* to subdue evil spirits."

Elijah considered this. "I can see that." For a moment we all sat in silence, observing the heavens. Then Lois ventured another yelp from inside the child trailer, followed by a sharp bark.

"Hold your horses there, Lois," Elijah called to her. He turned back to Brian. "I'd best be going. As you said, it's a long ways. Where are you two bound for?"

"Home," replied Brian.

"All right, then," said Elijah. "Safe journey."

"Safe journey to you, Elijah, and best of luck."

Elijah nodded, then remounted his bicycle and pedaled uncertainly off into the night.

"Hope he makes it all right," said Brian, starting up the car. "He looks pretty wobbly."

"Oh, he'll be fine. I guess I'd better start checking for flights out of Regina." I reached for my Zypad.

"Not much point in that." Brian checked for traffic – none, we and Elijah seemed to be the only living souls abroad that night – and pulled back onto the highway.

"But we've got to get Qianfu's bones to Vancouver as quickly as possible!"

"Let me paint you a picture, cuz. We arrive at airport security. The pre-board screening officer asks you to put your personal items through the scanner. 'Hold on, miss. What's that on the screen? I've never seen anything quite like that. I'm going to have to open that suit bag.'"

"But we could check it."

"They screen checked baggage too," he said. "They just don't do it in front of you."

He was right, of course. There was no way we could get a bag of bones on an airplane. "Well, then I guess we drive. I better tell Mom to call the rental agency in the morning, change the drop-off to Vancouver." Extracting my cell from my knapsack, I gave the voice command "Home" and enabled the speaker-phone function so that Brian could listen in. A second later, I heard the phone in the Pender Street house ring. It sounded so very far away, as though it lay at the bottom of a deep, deep well. It rang once, twice, three times . . .

"What time is it, anyway?" I asked Brian.

"Eleven."

"Maybe she's –"

A man answered. "Hello?"

At first I didn't recognize the voice. Maybe I had dialed a wrong number. But I'd given the right prompt. . . . Then I put two and two together.

"*Dad?* Dad, is that you?" I was beyond shocked. Dad hadn't answered a phone since his accident.

"David? What are you doing? Give me that," I heard a voice on the other end say, then my mother's voice on the line. "Hello. Who is this?"

"Miranda. It's me, Mom. Us. Brian and me."

"Who is it?" I heard my father say to my mother. He sounded confused, but he was talking. Talking! How long had it been since he'd uttered a coherent sentence? Months. Years.

"It's Miranda, David," my mother told him.

"Miranda? Who is Miranda?" He sounded agitated.

"Never mind, darling. Go sit down," she said to him. Then, "Where are you?" she asked me. "Have you been able to find out anything?"

Where to begin? I took a deep breath. "We're in Saskatchewan and, well, the long and the short of it is that we've got Qianfu's bones."

She gasped. "You're kidding! You actually did it? You actually found him?"

"Yup," I replied. "It took some sleuthing and some digging but, yeah, we found him and we're headed for home – by car, so we don't have to explain a bag of bones to airport security."

"Miranda? My daughter Miranda?" I heard in the background.

"Calm down, David! What's gotten into you?" I heard my mother say before my father wrestled the phone away from her. "It's ten o'clock, young lady. Why aren't you home?" he demanded, sounding almost like his old self.

"Oh, Daddy!" I burst into tears.

"Liam!" I heard my mother cry out. "What are you doing up? And what have you done with your nebulizer mask?" I heard insistent beeping. Mom snatched the phone from my father again. "The screen is showing call waiting from Sebastian at camp. At this hour? What is going on?"

The Grandfather is practicing *tai chi*, I thought. What I said was, "The beginning of the end, Mom. Only this time it's going to be a happy ending. You'll have to call the car rental place . . . let them know we'll be returning the car in Vancouver. We should be home" – I consulted the GPS's readout on the instrument panel – "in about eighteen hours, around five p.m. tomorrow if rush hour isn't too bad. The Grandfather said you would know what to do –"

"I do," she cut me off. "We've been ready for this for years, darling. Your grandmother and me. I know just what to do." There was a pause. "I am so proud of you . . . so proud of both of you." Her voice broke. "And so very grateful."

"Please, Mom," I begged. "Don't cry."

"You tell your cousin to drive safely," she said.

"He doesn't have a choice," I replied. "Speed lock."

"Thank goodness for that. Well, good night then. I love you."

Dad chimed in, "I love you too, but that doesn't mean you're not going to be punished for staying out late!"

"Right, Dad. I love you. Bye." I hung up, blinking back tears. "Did you hear that?" I asked Brian. "And Liam needs the nebulizer mask to breathe. He has for years. What's going on?"

"Things are happening, I guess," said Brian. "Forces are at work. The curse may not be good and lifted until Qianfu's bones are laid to rest in the cemetery, but in the meantime . . ." He grinned, then he frowned. "I just wish we could have saved my mom and dad."

"Me too." I gave his arm a squeeze.

We drove on in silence for a quarter of an hour before a green mileage sign swam into view. Swift Current, Medicine Hat, Calgary.

"So I'm going to be the geomancer in the family!" Brian savored the idea, patting the cherrywood box in his vest pocket. "Me . . . not you. Me."

"Give it a rest," I told him. "You'll wear it out."

"Not likely," he replied. "I'm going to be pretty powerful, you know. You might want to be nice to me."

"I *am* nice to you," I retorted.

"*Nicer*," he said. "Remember, I was going to save you from a shark."

"You were going to *try* and save me from a shark . . . and fail!"

"It's the thought that counts. A geomancer, eh? A geomancer!"

"It's going to be a long trip," I muttered. I settled back into my seat, folded my arms over my chest, and was about to close my eyes when Brian punched me in the arm.

"Ouch!"

"You know what, Randi?"

"What?"

He beamed at me. "This is going to be the best road trip ever! Can we stop for chips? Please! Please! I'm starving."

ACKNOWLEDGMENTS

I would like to thank the Ontario Arts Council for its ongoing support, my brother Peter Hardy, and my sister Pamela Rooks for their insightful critiques of early versions of this manuscript, and my agents Bill and Frances Hanna for all their hard work on my behalf. There are many reasons I wish Frances might have lived longer; one of them would have been so that she could see the fruits of her labors over many years. And, as always, thanks to my husband, Ken, who makes all things possible, including dogs.

ACKNOWLEDGMENTS

Melissa Hardy, a native of North Carolina, is the author of two collections of short stories, *Constant Fire* and *The Uncharted Heart*, and two novels, *A Cry of Bees* and *Broken Road*. The winner of the Journey Prize and the CAA's Silver Jubilee Award, Hardy's short fiction has been published in *The Atlantic Monthly*, among other magazines, and has been widely anthologized – twice in *Best American Short Stories* and *The Year's Best Fantasy and Horror*, and once in *Best Canadian Short Stories*. *The Geomancer's Compass* is her first young adult novel. Hardy makes her home in Port Stanley, Ontario, with her husband, Ken Trevenna, and Nellie, a golden retriever.